THE SPIDER:
SATAN'S SWITCHBOARD

THE MASTER OF MEN!
SPIDER®

SATAN'S SWITCHBOARD

By Grant Stockbridge

STEEGER BOOKS • 2021

CHAPTER 1
MARK OF THE SILENCER

"**L**ENORE!" THE name came in a shocked half-whisper from Nita van Sloan's lips; then immediately she regained her composure. Her lovely face lost its sudden alarm, and became expressionless except for the slightly narrowed eyes, the too taut set of her mouth, the telltale pallor of her cheeks. With well simulated calm she held the one-piece telephone to her ear—and carefully avoided Richard Wentworth's searching gaze.

But Wentworth had caught those unmistakable signs. He knew her so well that the attempt to disguise her agitation was useless. As the startled syllables still echoed in the quiet room, he was already rising from the table where they had been having lunch, springing across the apartment to an extension phone in the next room.

"He knows all about Earl!" a woman's voice, hysterical with terror, came to him, as he clamped the receiver to his ear. "I'm helpless, Nita, completely at his mercy—and he hasn't any mercy. Oh, I don't know *what* to do! You've *got* to help me, Nita. You know what to do in situations like this—you and Dick. Perhaps *he* will be able to do something!" New hope leaped into the pleading voice. "Please tell him, Nita—"

"Take hold of yourself, Lenore!" Nita's low, rich contralto was sharp and commanding despite its sympathetic warmth. "We'll

1

be there in a short while, but meanwhile I'll expect you to get yourself in hand. We'll figure some way to take care of you—don't worry about that!"

The phone clicked down on that note of reassurance, but, when Richard Wentworth stepped back into the main room and confronted her, he saw at a glance that the confidence she had tried to instill in Lenore Gleason was entirely synthetic. Nita was worried, and there were flickers of fear in the depths of her

Millions of dollars of gold would be snatched by the
Silencer in this perfectly executed robbery!

violet eyes. Lenore was one of her closest friends—a self-sufficient young woman not easily frightened—and yet the trouble that had engulfed her had reduced her to the verge of hysteria....

"You heard," Nita said simply. For a moment, her eyes met Wentworth's, locked with them in a glance of complete understanding—a flash of the perfect communion which these two had built up during years of facing peril side by side. "I've been afraid something like this would happen, sooner or later. I only hope it isn't...."

Her voice trailed off as if she did not dare put into words the thought that was stabbing at her mind. But Richard Wentworth understood, though his vital, flat-planed face, inscrutable as a mask, gave no sign of the fear that clutched at his heart.

"We'll be there in fifteen minutes," he said as he led the way from Nita's apartment in the Riverside Towers, and hailed a taxicab. "She undoubtedly is worked up—has been giving too much play to her imagination...."

But like Nita's his voice faded as he glanced out of the cab window and watched the snail's-pace at which they were traveling. Minutes counted now—even seconds might mean the difference between life and death. And as the taxi inched its way through maddening traffic, into Wentworth's mind leaped the memory of two other persons whose terror had not been the product of overworked imaginations... two others who had been reached too late.

The pressure of Nita's soft, warm fingers, closing around his hand, told him that she, too, remembered—and was shuddering at the grisly terror that she already pictured.

There was no response when they rang the bell of Lenore Gleason's apartment. Nita called her name, and Wentworth rapped his knuckles on the panel—without answer, there was only silence in the foyer, when he fitted a skeleton key to the lock and opened the door. They stood there, tense, every sense striving to pierce that wall of silence. Then Wentworth cat-footed forward, blocking Nita as she tried to dart past him.

At first glance, Lenore Gleason's living room seemed to be as empty as the foyer... and then they saw her, slumped in a heap on the floor, the telephone still clutched in one half-opened hand. But it was her face that riveted their attention—or what had been her face.

It was half-gone, skin eaten away to leave the raw, red flesh horribly exposed! Only her nose and the upper half of her face remained; beneath that, it was as if a huge hand had grabbed her from the rear, fastened its grip over her mouth to silence her—and then burned the impression of its constricting thumb and fingers deep into her seared flesh!

"The Silencer!" Nita gasped, as Wentworth tried to draw her away. "He's inhuman, Dick! He seems to find out everything!"

THE SILENCER, whose grisly, acid-eaten imprint listed Lenore Gleason as its latest victim, was the fiend whose ghastly exploits had been terrifying the city. As Wentworth stared down at the horribly disfigured face, he saw again those two other faces that had been similarly deformed—faces he and Nita had known well....

Ronald Boin, gay, wealthy, a favorite with both men and women, had been a man with everything to live for. Yet his valet had found him crumpled in an easy chair, an Egyptian dagger plunged into his heart. And when the corpse's head had lolled to one side, the valet had fainted… for the lower half of Boin's face was like raw beefsteak where the muffling fingers of the Silencer had closed over his lips and jaws!

The police had still been wrangling over Boin's death, still debating why his own fingerprints were on the hilt of the knife which had ended his life, as if he had committed suicide, while that ghastly disfigurement had obliterated half of his face—when they were called to stare, goggle-eyed, at the same gruesome trademark on the face of Mona Searles.

Lawrence Campbell, Mona's millionaire broker fiancé, had found the body. He had almost stumbled over it when he came through the terrace door of her penthouse… after she had failed to meet him at the elevator door. Mona Searles had been shot—shot twice with her own pearl-handled revolver. The weapon had been fired so close to her body that her dress was singed, her skin powder-marked. Suicide, pure and simple—except for that ghastly, flesh-raw hand that gripped the entire lower half of her face!

At first, those deaths—murders or suicides—had seemed inexplicable. But Wentworth's investigations had soon brought to light, in each case, compromising circumstances—closely guarded secrets supposedly known only to those directly concerned. Those secrets, he was convinced, had been discovered—and their discovery resulted in death....

His thoughts now flashed back to Lenore Gleason, who had reached trail's-end in less than fifteen minutes after her frantic plea for help. A socially prominent young heiress, Lenore had made the mistake of marrying a man who proved to be nothing more than a professional gambler. Systematically, Owen Gleason had drained her of money until, disillusioned, she had separated from him.

Since that time, she had fallen in love with Earl Hammond, vice president of the Colonial National Bank. But Gleason had laughed at her when she asked him for a divorce. Obdurately, he had stood in her way and blocked every attempt she made to gain freedom. Lenore had been extremely careful that Gleason should not learn about Earl Hammond, yet Wentworth recalled her frantic words over the wire, "He knows all about Earl." *Somebody* had discovered her secret—and then she had died.

That somebody was the Silencer!

Wentworth's face was grim, haggard, as he rose from his inspection.

RICHARD WENTWORTH'S deep-set, keen blue-gray eyes became hard and steely as he turned away from that pathetic corpse. His lean poker face was unchanged, but his tall, well poised figure, athletic shoulders and the purposeful stride of his lithe legs, bespoke the grim determination now blazing in his heart. For weeks, he had watched the crimson career of this criminal who called himself the Silencer, nerves tingling.

The apprehension of the Silencer was police business, but

the police were getting nowhere with it. Meanwhile, helpless victims were dying, desperately driven to suicide or murdered in cold blood. The great heart that had plucked Wentworth from a life of ease and luxury and set him to prowling the perilous byways

of the underworld, now gave him no rest. There was a task confronting him that he could no longer evade—a challenge to that relentless avenger whom men knew as the Spider.

And as he cast a last glance at Lenore Gleason's outraged face, Wentworth silently promised her that the Spider would not relinquish the grim trail until her murderer had paid the price with his own life!

Earl Hammond seemed to be the key to this tragedy. Somebody knew about Lenore's love for Hammond, and for that reason she had died. Perhaps the banker might possess some clue to this "somebody's" identity; Lenore might have confided in him before death stilled her lips. Certainly, Wentworth decided, Hammond ought to be interviewed, and that without delay.

"You will want to stay here with Lenore until the police arrive," he turned to Nita and his arm, around her slender waist, drew her close. "I want to have a talk with Earl Hammond. After that, I'll get in touch with you."

For a moment, her eyes searched his handsome, vital face. All too well she knew what those few words meant. Once more, the man, whom she loved with an intensity and understanding which is given to few women, was about to stake his life against the cunning of a diabolical murderer. Once more, Wentworth was about to don the black cape and hat, assume the repulsive face and straggly wig of the Spider, take the guise of the Nemesis of crime.

With all the fullness of her tender woman's love, she wanted to wrap her arms around him and hold him close—but that, she knew, was not Richard Wentworth's way. As her eyes flitted momentarily to the pitiful body of her friend, a sudden fierce pride surged into her heart for *her* man, for whom there could be no rest while the innocent and helpless suffered at the hands of ruthless criminal monsters.

"I shall be waiting to hear from you," she said softly; and for a moment her lips clung to his before she let him depart....

CHAPTER 2
DEATH'S TRAIL

THE COLONIAL National Bank was located on one of the narrow lanes that constitute the catacombs of Manhattan's financial district. It was shortly after two when Wentworth picked his way through the crowd and approached the wide entrance. A towel-supply truck, he noticed subconsciously, was drawn up in the cleared space at the curb beside a side door, the driver hopping out and striding toward its rear.

Wentworth passed beside it to reach the sidewalk, and then he was climbing the broad stone steps, walking across the marble floor and approaching that section of the bank roped off for the desks and offices of the executives. Hammond was not in evidence, and Wentworth stepped up to a secretary to inquire for him—when suddenly the girl's eyes bulged and her mouth dropped open… She trembled.

In the same instant, a pall of silence seemed to fall over the interior of the bank, a hushed quiet made all the more impressive by the pandemonium raging outside!

Like statues, figures suddenly frozen into immobility, the tellers stood in their cages; wide-eyed, ashen-faced, the customers, lined up at the windows, seemed bereft of all life. In mid-stride the activity of that great financial institution had suddenly stopped as if the dynamo which operated it had ceased functioning—and outside the narrow street reverberated with the rattle of machine-gun fire!

A split-second Wentworth stood there like the others, then flashed into action. Whirling where he stood, his leap carried him halfway to the door. His automatics were in his hands, as he raced down the steps and into the street, turning instinctively to where that towel-supply truck was backed against the curb.

Now the rear of the truck was open, revealing its true nature. Instead of the ordinary commercial vehicle it had appeared, it was actually an armored truck. Four guards had stepped from its interior—and now lay sprawled on the street that was splashed with their blood. From the protection of the shatterproof-glassed driver's seat, a lone survivor was putting up a desperate defense. But even as Wentworth's feet landed on the sidewalk, the glass crumpled under the battering of a high-caliber sub-machine gun, and the face of the guard became a bloody horror.

The men in that truck had never had a chance, Wentworth saw at once. A withering hail of bullets had been hosed into them from the cars parked on either side of the cleared space, while sharpshooters blazed away at them from half a dozen other points.

Their weapons still spitting lead, these masked killers swooped down on the dead men and grabbed the heavy canvas sacks their victims had been carrying—sacks handcuffed to their wrists. Momentarily, razor-sharp meat axes flashed in the air... and four severed hands lay on the sidewalk as the thieves seized the sacks and tossed them to others who waited at the doors of their cars.

Then they were leaping into the truck, tossing out other sacks and metal-bound boxes, while the deadly snouts of the machine guns from the protecting cars kept the frightened bystanders at a distance.

The moment Wentworth sprang out into the street, one of those watchful gunmen spied him. The tommy-gun chattered its death-song, spraying the side of the bank with bullets, as Wentworth flung himself down behind the protection of a stone pillar at the side of the steps. Flat on his belly, Wentworth tried to return that fire. One of the thugs at the open door of the truck screamed in agony, and pitched to the sidewalk—and at that moment a young policeman came diving through the crowd.

Magnificent fool! He never had a chance. The deadly scything lead cut him down before he could fire a shot, and with him sent a dozen terror-paralyzed bystanders to the sidewalk, moaning in their death agony.

Wentworth's teeth gritted at the shrill screams of a girl, who had been cut almost in two by the blasting lead. It knifed into his brain! Deliberately, he picked his man—and another thug toppled out of the open door of the truck and crashed, face down, onto the sidewalk.

But the death of two of their number had no effect whatsoever on the others. Like a smoothly oiled machine, they worked. The hold-up had been carefully planned, timed to perfection—and nothing was being allowed to interfere with it. In less than two minutes after the first shot had signalized the attack, the truck was looted, the killers were in the cars and the drivers stepping on the gas.

But when the last of the killers sprang through the open car door, Wentworth leaped from cover, grabbed at him. He clung to the thug's arm with one hand while his automatic swung at the masked face. Then a hard fist smashed against his jaw, dazed him. He lost his footing, toppled from the running-board…but, before he fell, his fingers clutched wildly at that black mask, ripped it away….

In that flashing glimpse, before the car swept away with the killer, Wentworth recognized his adversary. It was Sam Latshaw, a murderer for whom the police now scoured the city!

BY THE time Wentworth picked himself up from the gutter, both cars had sped around a corner, lost in the Broadway traffic a few blocks away. With danger past, the gaping bystanders were coming to their senses. The street was jammed with curious onlookers, pressing close to view the bullet-torn corpses that littered the sidewalk.

Unobtrusively, Wentworth edged his way through the crowd until he was back at the bank's main entrance. Uniformed guards were now barricading the doors, as if to withstand a fresh assault. One of them consented to take in Wentworth's card when he insisted upon seeing Earl Hammond.

A few minutes later, the guard was back and Wentworth was being led inside—but not to Earl Hammond's office. Instead, he was escorted to the elegant quarters where Giles Norton, president of the bank, sat glowering behind his big desk.

"Mr. Wentworth?" The banker glanced up. "I know of you— from Earl Hammond and from Commissioner Kirkpatrick. You had an appointment with Mr. Hammond this afternoon?"

Before Wentworth could answer, Norton was on his feet, leading the way to another office. Dramatically, he opened the closed door—and Wentworth stared at the limp figure of Earl Hammond slumped in his desk chair, a long, Oriental-looking knife plunged almost to the hilt into his left breast!

"I was talking to him five minutes ago," Norton was babbling. "He seemed perfectly all right, then—perfectly happy. He was coming out to my Westchester place for the week-end. The moment the shooting started outside, he must have killed himself. I can't understand it, Wentworth! Why a man like Hammond should—"

Wentworth leaned over the body, examining it. From the position into which the right hand had fallen, he knew that its fingers had been around the hilt of the knife; Hammond's fingerprints would be on it. Another seemingly clear case of suicide. When he stooped and picked up a crumpled piece of paper that lay on the floor at the dead man's feet, the last vestige of doubt seemed to evaporate.

Wentworth flattened out that square of paper and stared down at a typewritten note which read—

> Everything arranged. Tomorrow, the 24th, at 2:10. Plans perfected so that you need have no fear of a slip-up. We do not fail!

And beneath those damning lines was a rubber-stamped signature—a line drawing representation of a man's head, the eyes fairly bulging out of their sockets as a hand from behind him clamped over his mouth and gagged him. It was the signature of the Silencer!

Giles Norton looked at that note, and the last traces of color drained from his face.

"The Silencer!" he whispered. "Hammond—Hammond was working with the Silencer! That shipment we just lost contained a quarter million dollars in cash and securities. I thought we had it perfectly covered, disguised—but the Silencer found out about it! Somehow, he knew—"

Wentworth had recrumpled the note and dropped it back onto the floor where he had found it. Urging Norton out of the door, and closing it behind them so that nothing should be disturbed when the homicide-squad men arrived, he led the way back to the president's office. Keenly, he watched Norton, as the trembling banker dropped into his desk chair.

"Somebody betrayed us," he was mumbling almost to himself. "Somebody sold us out to the Silencer—but it *couldn't* have been Hammond," his voice rose agitatedly. "Hammond didn't know when that shipment was to arrive—couldn't have known. I was the only one who knew. I arranged it with Luther Pollard, general manager of the Federal Trucking—by telephone not more than two hours ago. Even the men on the truck didn't know what they were carrying. But the Silencer *knew!* He knew exactly when to have his crooks here—"

Suddenly, Norton whirled in his chair and his pallid face flushed angrily.

"Nobody knew what was in that shipment, or when it would arrive, but Pollard and myself," he repeated. "Nobody else could have known—unless someone listened in on our conversation. The only one who could have done that was the switchboard operator! That's the answer, Wentworth!" He thumped his fist on his desk, and the red veins stood out at his temples. "It's that damned operator! That explains a great deal that's been puzzling me lately—explains other leaks here in the bank!"

ABRUPTLY, HE grabbed up his phone and barked an order for the operator to come to his office at once. The moment she stepped through the doorway, he pounced upon her.

"I suppose you want to know why I called you here, Miss Rice?" he snarled. "Well, your spying and double-crossing is finished. We know how those thieves found out exactly when the Federal truck would deliver the shipment I arranged with Luther Pollard. We know that you listened in on my telephone conversation, and passed the word along to your confederates.

You've been listening in for weeks, selling the information you picked up—"

Wentworth's eyes flicked from Norton's flushed face to the girl. Slim, pretty, with blue eyes and red-gold hair, she flinched back from those viciously flung charges as if lashed across the face with a whip. For a moment on the verge of tears, her lips clenched firmly, angry eyes returning Norton's glare.

"That isn't true, Mr. Norton!" she protested vehemently. "You have no right to say that. I have been with the bank more than five years and there never has been any question about my integrity. I haven't time to listen in on your calls, even if I wanted to! I haven't any confederates—"

Giles Norton wasn't listening to her. His fingers were tapping on the desk, and Wentworth could fairly see the wheels of his mind going round, knitting a web of guilt that would enmesh the girl.

Wentworth's shrewd eyes had been appraising the banker from the moment they met, and he had missed none of the furtiveness, guilty uneasiness, which had characterized the man. But now that was gone, given away before a flood of vindictive assurance. Giles Norton, he knew, was concealing something that had him worried frantic—something from which he was desperately seeking relief in damning this girl.

"I'm not interested in anything you have to say," Norton snapped. "There will be plenty of time for that when you come up before a judge. You're going to be arrested as an accessory in this robbery, the moment the police get here. I'll prefer charges that will keep you tucked away in jail until they round up the rest of your gang—"

Before he could finish, the door of his office opened, and in strode a bushy-haired young fellow of twenty-five or six, wearing the gray alpaca office coat standard in the bank. His eyes were blazing, lips drawn back tight against his teeth as he glanced around the office and centered his contemptuous gaze on Norton.

"You dirty, rotten philanderer!" he flung at the bank president. "You're looking for a scapegoat, are you? You'll make Mabel take the rap for you? Well, you won't get away with it, Norton. Nobody has to listen in on your wire to know what a rotter you are. If anybody tipped off those crooks, it was you!"

"York!" Norton barked. "You must be crazy—unless, by God, you had a hand in this thing yourself!"

"No—he didn't!" the girl sprang forward impulsively. "He couldn't have, Mr. Norton—you know that! Oh, Phil, you'll—" she turned her eyes to the fuming clerk—"you'll get yourself in trouble!"

"Keep out of this, Mabel," York clipped. "I'm not letting them put a frame-up like this over on you. Never mind pushing that buzzer, Norton. I'll get out of your lousy bank and stay out. But I'll settle this score with you—don't forget that. And with this cheap dick too." He whirled on Wentworth. "You couldn't wait until the regular cops come, could you? You had to bring this fellow in and pay him to back up your lies—"

Two husky bank guards had answered Norton's buzzer and

17

were dragging the young fellow out of the office, but in the doorway he braced himself and turned on Wentworth.

"A fine specimen of man you are!" he spat scornfully. "Persecuting a helpless girl for a few dirty dollars!"

And then the door closed behind him, and the silence in the office was broken only by Mabel Rice's sobs....

CHAPTER 3
SILENCE BEFORE SLAYING

POLICE COMMISSIONER Stanley Kirkpatrick had been using every resource of his department to trap the criminal who was operating under the guise of the Silencer—and the result of his best efforts had been absolutely nothing, while the list of known victims steadily grew longer. Attacked by the newspapers, always quick to feature crimes with such a sensational angle, he was at his wit's end; so Wentworth had little doubt of how he would receive the news of these latest outrages.

"It gets worse and worse, Dick." His handsome, florid face was lined with worry, as he brushed the first knuckle of his right hand back and forth across his spiked mustache. "This makes six bodies that have been found with the faces half-eaten away by that hellish mark. During the past three months, there has been an alarming increase in the number of suicides among well-to-do people—people who apparently had no reason in the world for doing away with themselves."

"If they *were* suicides," Wentworth amended, but Kirkpatrick shook his head wearily.

"Some of them had to be," he insisted. "I'll grant that the hand-marked ones may have been murders, but the others... Daily, the robberies and hold-ups pile up," he resumed his doleful inventory. "They are utterly baffling because they are timed so perfectly and executed without a slip. I've had sufficient police experience to know that an outbreak of this sort is not the result of coincidence. These crimes are related, all part of a deliberate campaign—and the devil behind them is this Silencer!"

Kirkpatrick seemed to have aged during the past few weeks. A well set-up man in his late forties, immaculately dressed even to the gardenia in his buttonhole, there was about him the dignity and authority which came with years of command. But now his eyes were haggard, and there was a slump to his square shoulders that betrayed the pressure under which he had been laboring.

"This Colonial National hold-up makes three of the largest banks in the city that have been victimized," he finished. "Perfect jobs, every one of them. In ten minutes, I'm having a conference here—the three bank presidents, and Pollard from the Federal Trucking Company. Wait until they arrive, and maybe we'll be able to put our fingers on some sort of lead that will get us somewhere." He slumped back.

Wentworth waited—and hoped against hope that the commissioner's conference might prove worth while. Kirkpatrick and he had been through years of crime-fighting together, facing deadly peril side by side so often that each held a profound respect for the other—a feeling augmented by a genuine friendship.

Often their methods were at variance—especially when Wentworth, realizing the limitations of regular police methods, donned the somber vestments of the Spider and fought beyond-the-law crooks in the only way they could be mastered. Stern and uncompromising, Kirkpatrick was a symbol of the law and would tolerate no man's taking police powers into his own hands, even though the ends to be gained were the same for which he strove himself.

For years, he had more than suspected that Richard Wentworth was the Spider, that shadowy figure the mere mention of whose name sent the underworld rats scurrying to their holes; but never had the actual proof of that suspicion fallen into his hands. If ever that day arrived, he had sworn that he would deliver the Spider up to justice, even though that might mean sending him to the electric chair.

Moreover, Wentworth knew that he would keep his word—and respected him for it. On that mutual respect and understanding, they had built a friendship such as comes to few men....

WENTWORTH SINCERELY hoped that the commissioner's conference might prove productive, but he had little faith in the meeting. Five minutes after the bankers were gathered around Kirkpatrick's conference table, he knew that his pessimism was justified. None of the executives had anything to contribute which had not already been revealed. Each admitted that the hold-up at his bank had been perfectly timed, perfectly engineered, and evidently based upon inside information which should have been inviolate.

In each case, every precaution had been taken to keep secret the presence of an unusually large amount of cash and securities, and in each case the Silencer had known just when to strike. In each case, one of the bank officers was found dead, an apparent suicide—though the victim had supposedly been in ignorance of the arrangements until the shipment arrived and the hold-up was staged.

"These men could not have known the information that was passed over to the Silencer, and yet they seemed to have committed suicide because of their guilty connection with him," Wentworth summed up. "Obviously, these notes, and the deaths themselves, were blinds, gentlemen—blinds to cover up the real source of information by means of which the Silencer is able to operate. There is a leak somewhere in your organizations. Mr. Norton suspects his switchboard operator. How about the rest of you?"

"My operator has been with me for fifteen years," Luther Pollard announced immediately. "She is as much a part of Federal Trucking as I am—and I would no more suspect her than myself. The leak isn't on our end. You may be sure of that."

"That puts it up to the banks—and means that all three operators would have to have been corrupted," Wentworth pointed out.

"Not mine," Frederick Spalding, of the Farmers and Furriers, was equally emphatic; and Raymond Tuttle, of the Merchants'

Exchange, chimed in with unqualified endorsement of his operator.

Only Giles Norton nodded his head in assent.

"I've found the leak, so far as we are concerned," he ground out his words with vindictive relish. "I should have suspected her before. But when the police start sweating her, we'll be on the track of Mr. Silencer—don't worry about that."

Again Wentworth watched him keenly and sensed the fear that was beneath the man's bluster. Again he realized that Giles Norton was frantic to hide something that had been torturing him and to find someone to blame for it. And Mabel Rice was the someone he had chosen....

THE CONFERENCE broke up without success, but as the bankers departed Wentworth's brain was busily organizing the information and impressions he had gathered. The switchboard operators, with the exception of Mabel Rice, seemed to be in the clear; and the final arrangements for the looted shipments, each executive had testified, had been made by telephone. That meant that the leak, if there was one, must be in the central offices of the telephone company.

At least that was a lead worth following, and Wentworth decided to take it up at once with his friend, Arthur Morrell,

RICHARD
WENTWORTH

the telephone company's general manager.

"One of our girls listening in and relaying messages?" Morrell frowned when Wentworth, seated in his private office, had explained the purpose of his call. "That's a pretty far-fetched idea. These banks are located in two exchange districts," he checked up. "That means at least two operators must be involved—and probably three, because it would be too much of a coincidence if one girl had handled the calls from two of the banks at just the right time to pick up this information. Besides, you have a dozen or more other crimes you blame on the Silencer—which means that he would have to have agents in the exchanges all over the city. You're barking up the wrong tree, Dick. Our girls have far too much work to handle to allow them time for eavesdropping."

"If it isn't the girls, how about wire-tappers?" Wentworth hazarded. "Any way they could operate in the exchange?"

"None," Morrell denied. "The only way wiretapping can be managed is on the subscriber's end, after his wire leaves the cables—and that would mean dozens of wire-tappers busy all over the city. Surely one of them would have been caught by now. So far as wire-tapping in the exchanges is concerned, that's out. We don't tolerate anything of that sort—even from the police. In fact, I fired one of our laboratory men a while ago simply because we found him experimenting with a contraption that would make some sort of wire-tapping possible."

"Who was that fellow—do you remember his name?" Wentworth pounced on that bit of information eagerly.

Morrell pursed his lips and stared out of the window thoughtfully.

"Why, yes." He swiveled back to Wentworth. "He was—"

Like the sound of a book suddenly being snapped shut, something popped behind Wentworth's back—and Arthur Morrell clutched at his breast as he half rose from his chair, only to crumple and sprawl on the broad top of his desk. The death gurgle was in his throat, drowning the half-moan on his lips, as Wentworth leaped to his side and tried to raise him.

In the same split-second, the side door of the office snapped shut—and the click of its latch was echoed by another *pop* of a silenced automatic, the crash of splintering glass!

Swiftly, Wentworth leaped from the lifeless body of his friend and was at the side door, yanking it open, to fling himself into the adjoining office and stare at the body of Warner Keller, the assistant general manager, slumped, like his chief, over the glass top of his desk. Keller's eyes were closed, his mouth was half-open, fingers half-hooked as if clutching vainly for a grip on the smooth glass.

At the farther end of Keller's office was the partitioned-off cubicle that was the quarters of Vincent Crosby, his male secretary. The door stood open, and the pane of glass, which ran from three feet above the floor to the ceiling, hung in jagged shards in its frame.

These things Wentworth catalogued in the flash of an eye. Then he saw Crosby at the door which led from Keller's sanctum to the general office outside. The secretary pulled the door open and stood swaying drunkenly, fumbling blindly for the jamb as a cloud of grayish smoke billowed in and enveloped him.

For a moment, Crosby stood reeling there. Then he seemed to go into a weird dervish dance, a wild corkscrewing that twisted his legs beneath him and fairly melted him to the floor.

Too late, Wentworth realized the meaning of that blue-gray smoke. Too late, he whirled and tried to run to a window. The expanding smoke cloud shot out tenuous fingers that wrapped around him, clutched at his throat, throttled his windpipe. Uncertainly, he stumbled forward, gasping for air, as his head swam sickeningly—and then something within his brain seemed to explode. Frightful pain radiated from the top of his skull. He was falling, falling through endless space, stifling darkness....

For countless ages, he seemed to be wallowing through that darkness, then to be climbing up through it—until he opened his smarting eyes and found himself on knees and hands, frantically trying to get to his feet. The gas had lifted somewhat, and currents of fresh air were swirling into the office.

The window—he must get that window open! But it *was* open. Only then did he see Vincent Crosby's nearly bald head raise over the sill, as the middle-aged, mild-mannered secretary straightened and staggered across the office to open another window. Crosby had been the first to recover consciousness, open that window and lean out to gulp in eager breaths of fresh, strength-restoring air....

WHEN WENTWORTH groped his way to Keller's desk, the assistant manager was just coming to his senses. With a low moan, he leaned back in his chair and held both hands to his temples. There seemed to be no blood upon him or evidence of a wound other than the swelling on the back of his head that he was tenderly massaging.

"I don't know a thing," he groaned, when Wentworth tried to question him. "I was sitting here, working—and suddenly my skull seemed to split wide open. It felt as if the ceiling had come down on my head. That's the last I remember until I found myself lying there on the glass. What in hell happened?"

That was what Wentworth wanted to know. As soon as he saw that Keller could furnish no information, he started across the room to the outer door office. Vincent Crosby was there ahead of him, throwing open windows and trying to revive the half-dozen clerks who lay on the floor or crumpled over their desks.

One by one, they came back to consciousness, but they knew little more than Keller. They had been at work and had suddenly noticed that the air was thick and stifling, that they could not draw their breaths—and then they had slipped away into oblivion.

Only Crosby had actually seen the killer who had stalked through those offices, and his voice trembled so at the memory that he could barely make himself understood.

"I heard that shot—it sounded like something that had fallen down or broken," he chattered. "I ran out of my office to see what had happened—and there in the doorway of Mr. Morrell's office was a man with an automatic in his hand. He had a queer-looking mask over his whole face and his felt hat was pulled down low over his forehead—but I could see him snarling at me through the glass eyes in the thing. Mr. Keller was lying there at his desk, as if dead—and when that fellow pointed his gun at me, I thought my time had come.

"He shot, and the bullet smashed the glass right alongside my head. I don't know how it missed me. I must have ducked just in time; and when I picked myself up he was running through the door into the general office. I tried to follow him, but the gas knocked me out as soon as I opened the door."

A murderer armed with a silenced automatic and a gas mask! Somehow, he had managed to flood the outer office with suffocating gas, come in and knocked out Keller, and then shot Morrell from the doorway of Keller's office. Wentworth pieced the thing together as he started back to the general manager's quarters and opened the door.

The body of Arthur Morrell was lying half-sprawled over his desk, just as it had been. But the moment Wentworth glanced at it he could feel the blood chilling in his veins. Somebody had been in that office since Morrell died—somebody whose searing hand had closed over the general manager's mouth and burned its way into his flesh!

His face was half-gone, the skin and flesh of the lower half eaten away in the familiar dread pattern of a clutching hand! Clasped in his dead fingers was a typewritten card which Wentworth gingerly removed—

MEDDLERS

This is the reward of a wagging tongue. The same fate is in store for you if you make any attempt to interfere with—

And beneath the typewritten lines was the grisly rubber-stamped drawing that was the signature of the Silencer!

CHAPTER 4
TIGHTENING WEB

WHEN RICHARD Wentworth left the telephone company building, he sensed that he was being watched—that hidden eyes were spying on him, following his every movement. Twice, he was sure that he detected shadows trailing him, and he had eluded them. But now there was no doubt in his mind that the Silencer had become aware of his existence. Plainly, that warning card in Morrell's dead hand had been meant for him. The Silencer had thrown down the gauntlet to Richard Wentworth.

But, while the Silencer knew him, Wentworth had not even a suspicion of the master criminal's identity. There were only two leads which might guide him to the fellow—Owen Gleason, Lenore's husband, and Sam Latshaw, the fugitive killer.

Latshaw undoubtedly could point the way to the man who directed his movements. Where to find Latshaw was another matter. Gleason, too, might know the Silencer's identity or even be working with him. He might have supplied the information which had set the Silencer on Lenore's trail. That much would be quite in keeping with Gleason's character....

From a telephone booth, Wentworth called the gambler and asked for an interview with him—a request which Gleason promptly granted. He invited Wentworth to come right up to his apartment, and was waiting almost at the door when his caller arrived.

"I suppose you have come to see me because of Lenore," he suggested, ushering Wentworth to a comfortable chair and wheeling up a well stocked portable bar beside it. "Ghastly thing, wasn't it? I've already been to headquarters and assured the police that I am ready to do anything in my power to help them catch her murderer—if she was murdered."

Wentworth poured himself a brandy, and, over the top of his glass, studied the thin-faced, sleek-haired gambler who, he recognized, was watching him as intently as he doubtless had ever regarded any of his victims across the gaming tables. Gleason was handsome, dashing—but there was also an over-effusiveness about him, an artificial cordiality, that instinctively aroused Wentworth's distrust.

"Lenore and I had our quarrels," Gleason smiled knowingly. "In some ways, we didn't quite see eye to eye, so to speak. But my affection for her never changed. If the police find the man who killed her—the dirty devil who disfigured her face—I want a few minutes alone with him before they take him away. Just a few minutes, man to man—that's all I ask, Wentworth!"

Now he was striding up and down the lavishly furnished living-room like an over-dramatic actor, slim-fingered hands knotting into fists and then unclenching as he picked up and lit a fresh cigarette, only to discard it after a few puffs. Giving a fine portrayal of a bereaved and distraught husband, Wentworth noted—but the performance was insincere, unconvincing,

entirely for effect. Or was there something more than that behind it?

That suspicion grew in Wentworth's
mind, as the minutes passed—as Gleason deftly parried every question which
was too pertinent or might have proved
embarrassing. He was giving no worth-
while information—yet obviously was
prolonging the interview, dragging it out by long-winded remi-
niscences of no consequence. And always his dark, restless eyes
seemed watching... and waiting!

Gleason wasn't a good gambler—that had always been his
trouble. He wasn't a good actor, either. He overplayed his role
so badly that Wentworth sensed a trap—that he was being held
here until everything should be in readiness. That subconscious
forewarning, alone saved his life when he left the apartment....

ALERTLY, HIS eyes flashed up and down the corridor
the moment he stepped out into the hall. There was nobody
there—or waiting when he cautiously edged around a right-an-
gle turn and walked to the elevator. But the moment the shaft
door opened, and he stepped into the car, every nerve in his
body tingled.

Unintentionally, the elevator boy gave the thing away. His
face, tense and set, was almost drained of color, nostrils distended
fearfully. He could not conceal the trembling of his fingers, as he
fumbled with the door. He was like a man who expects, at any
moment, to hear a terrific explosion....

In the same fractional second, Wentworth glimpsed the other

The trap had been carefully planned for moment Wentworth came out of Gleason's apartment!

occupant of the car, standing at one side, not more than a foot
from the operator. About thirty, swarthy-faced, the man wore
a brown felt hat snapped down over his eyes, a light brown

topcoat, unbuttoned—and his hands were thrust into the coat pockets.

The car started down, hesitantly—as if the operator were loath to finish the trip. One floor, another... Then it stopped, and he pushed back the gate, although Wentworth had noticed that there were no other stops signaled on the indicator. The shaft door swung open, and in came another slouching individual with his hands in pockets. This one stepped to the rear of the car.

Wentworth caught the gleam of perspiration on the operator's hand, as he gripped the control and resumed the downward trip. Sweat beaded out on the attendant's forehead, as he stood there stiff as a poker, staring straight ahead of him. The car slowed for the main floor. Like an automaton, the operator's hand reached out for the gate, for the shaft door, swung it wide—to flinch back against his controls as if he expected all hell to come rushing in at him.

Wentworth hesitated, muscles tense, ready. Neither of his fellow passengers started for the open door. Then he noticed the right-hand pocket's bulge, rising, pointing significantly in his direction. Beneath the snap-brim hat, he caught a glimpse of sardonic eyes, their corners half-puckered in a mocking leer.

Deliberately, Wentworth reached into his vest pocket and took out a cigarette case... while that brown pocket bulge sharpened and pointed straight at his middle. Calmly, he slid out a cigarette and put it into his mouth, slipped the case back into his pocket and struck a match, puffed until he had a light.

The match was still blazing between his fingers as he stepped out into the lobby, bent to thrust it into the sand jar beside the elevator—and with the same motion galvanized into action!

The brown-coated individual was right at his heels—so close that the heavy sand jar, suddenly overturning, caught him across the shins and sent him staggering back into the car with a yell of pain and surprise. Through that pocket bulge, a gun roared harmlessly. The lobby was filled with the smell of burned cloth, as a handful of the scooped-up sand flew into the car and dashed into the eyes of the second gunman.

Before the swarthy killer could get his weapon out of his smoldering pocket, Wentworth was flat on the floor, rolling to the protection of a pillar. At the street door a gun roared, and a bullet spat against the composition-stone flooring within inches of his head. There were two more of the gang there in the doorway, he saw. But now his automatics were in his hands—and one of his new adversaries dropped to the floor, holding his belly and writhing in agony.

Both of those deadly guns were blazing, filling the little lobby with their thunder; and once more the uncanny accuracy which Richard Wentworth had developed, by long hours of target practice, stood him in good stead. Swarthy-face's gun roared, but, even as his finger released the trigger, a round black hole appeared just over the bridge of his nose and he wilted to the floor.

Out of the elevator leaped the remaining gunman, still rubbing at his smarting, half-blinded eyes. He could not see to shoot accurately, but his hurtling leap carried him halfway to where Wentworth crouched, and his heavy automatic was raised over his head to smash down in a skull-splintering blow. Before he could accomplish that, two of his would-be victim's bullets caught him in mid-stride and hurled him back against the elevator doorway, to slump in a heap at the foot of the retching operator.

Wentworth had only time to flash a glance at the street doorway, but, instinctively, he wriggled into a position that partially protected him from a cross-fire from that quarter. After that first bullet had slapped against the floor, only two others came seeking him. They thudded into the pillar beside him, showering him with powdered plaster. Then, abruptly, silence settled over the lobby… silence broken only by terrified wheezing of the operator and the dying moan of the swarthy-faced killer.

Wentworth's sharp ears picked out the pound of running feet, the roar of an accelerating motor. That fourth killer was making his getaway!

Wentworth scrambled to his feet and raced across the short lobby, but the fleeing car was already halfway down the block. A wild shot spat at him from its side window, and then it had reached the corner and swung out of sight.

THOUGHTFULLY, HE walked to the corner and hailed a cab, gave the driver the address of his Sutton Place residence. Four killers and a waiting sedan! He would have been shot down in that lobby or carried off in the car to be dumped out, lifeless, somewhere in a deserted spot, he considered, as the taxi sped him across town. The trap had been carefully timed for the moment he came out of Owen Gleason's apartment. But there was not a thing to connect the gambler with it, no matter what his own conviction might be. Gleason was in the clear, yet—more than ever, Wentworth sensed that the fellow was in some way tied up with the Silencer....

But for the moment there was nothing more to be learned from him, and already Wentworth's churning thoughts were spreading in other directions, making other plans.

There seemed to be no pursuit or eyes spying on him, when he dismissed the driver in front of the Sutton Place apartment house in which he kept a lower floor suite. Nobody was in the lobby when he crossed to a rear door and unlocked it. Once inside, he went straight to a bedroom closet that was filled with clothes, pressed a button that wafted the clothing to one side and opened a side wall of the cubicle to reveal a stairway leading down to a concrete tunnel. At the end of that tunnel was the veritable fortress that was the home of Richard Wentworth, the attack-proof lair of the Spider.

With a word of greeting to the three faithful retainers whose devotion to him made them far more than servants, he went to his living-room and dialed Nita van Sloan's number. Her response was immediate—and Wentworth knew that she had been waiting anxiously for that call. Briefly, he narrated what had occurred at the Colonial Bank and the telephone company, and then confided his suspicions of Owen Gleason.

"That Rice girl doesn't strike me as guilty," he came back to the arrest of the Colonial Bank switchboard operator. "There is something more to Norton's vindictiveness than he is admitting, and she may help us to uncover it. I want you to bail her out, Nita. Then contact the operator in Gleason's place. Offer

37

her a vacation with pay if she will play sick for a week or two and maneuver Mabel Rice in as her substitute at the board. I want a report on every call that goes over Gleason's wire."

Wentworth hung up after Nita had assured him that she would be able to negotiate the substitution. The instrument was hardly back in its cradle, when the bell clamored for attention. A man's voice, hoarse and excited, came over the wire.

"This is Giles Norton, Wentworth," it babbled frantically. "I must see you, man! I must see you at once. Please come up here to my place. I *must* talk to you! I'll pay anything you say—any fee you name—but it's imperative that I see you without delay."

Wentworth agreed, and Norton gasped with relief. The trail was getting warmer, and Wentworth's blood tingled with anticipation as he arose from his desk and went to his private bathroom. For a moment, he stood undecided. Then his fingers touched a succession of the colored tiles in one of the walls, and part of that wall slid back to reveal a compact dressing-room— equipped with dressing-table and neon-lighted mirror, with makeup kit and supplies.

Thoughtfully, he lifted from a hook a long black cape and a soft, floppy black hat that would come down over a straggly black wig. A few minutes at that table and his deft fingers would transform his handsome face into the ugly countenance of the Spider—a creature of sallow complexion, discolored, snaggly teeth, bushy brows and ugly, deep-lined cheeks. A twisted, stooping creature swathed in the black of the night that was his natural habitat….

But Wentworth shook his head and replaced the ebon cloak.

This Silencer was no ordinary criminal; his preparations were too careful, too foolproof. Before he was throttled, every resource of the Spider might have to be utilized—and the time for that was not yet. First, Wentworth must have something more definite on which to work.

And Giles Norton ought to be able to furnish that.

IT WAS only a few minutes' ride to the East Sixty-second Street mansion that was Giles Norton's home. Wentworth did not bother using his own car. He took a taxi, and peered out of the window as the cab turned into the banker's block.

That four-story building, with the white, marble lower floor, was Norton's. There was a light in the vestibule that made the white portals gleam in the dusk. Wentworth reached into his pocket for his wallet—and suddenly tensed on the seat, his eyes glued on that entranceway. Then he had the door open, was leaping out onto the sidewalk and racing down the street, to throw his arms around a figure that had darted furtively from the white-fronted building and started to run down the block.

The fellow struggled frantically the moment he felt that grip around his shoulders, tried desperately to wriggle out of the imprisoning arms that wrapped around him—but now one of his wrists was snared. Vise-like fingers closed around it and twisted his arm behind his back. All the resistance went out of him.

With a frenzied curse, he relaxed, bent forward and twisted around—so that Wentworth could peer into the anguished face of young Phil York! Why had York—

Fresh terror flooded that face the moment the bank clerk recognized his captor.

"I haven't done anything—you haven't got anything on me!" he protested fearfully. "You can't frame me the way you did Mabel—I haven't done anything, I tell you! Let me go! You're breaking my arm!" as the pressure increased.

"What were you doing there in Norton's house?" Wentworth demanded.

"I wasn't..." York denied, but the agony of his twisted arm changed his mind. "He sent for me—he wanted to see me. I just came to talk to him."

"Then we'll go back inside and finish the conversation," Wentworth decided, as he dragged his captive over to the taxi while he paid the driver and then started toward the white doorway.

York had given up his attempts to escape, but his face was pale and his eyes gleamed with terror, as he mounted the steps. Wentworth could feel his body stiffening, his muscles becoming taut.

There was no response to the bell, so Wentworth tried the door. It opened to his touch—but that was the signal for York to make a last desperate attempt to get away. Flat on the floor he dropped and tried to turn a somersault so as to free his tortured arm. But Wentworth was prepared for that. His grip tightened inexorably, until York clambered to his knees and crawled through the doorway, into the hallway, past the wide arch of the empty reception-room.

Wentworth paused, and listened. There wasn't a sound in the

house. Nobody seemed to have heard their entrance. It was as if the place were deserted.

"Where is Norton?" he demanded as he hauled his captive to his feet.

"Back—back there," York whimpered, and with the snout of an automatic digging into the small of his back he led the way to a room at the rear of the building.

In the doorway of that room, he hesitated and seemed to lose all motive power. Frightened, inarticulate words were spilling from his lips, but Wentworth brushed him aside and snapped on the lights—to stare down at the outstretched body of Giles Norton. The banker was lying on his back, a stiletto standing upright in the breast of his blood-reddened shirt—and the lower half of his face eaten away in the raw-flesh mark of the Silencer!

"I didn't do it!" York finally found his tongue. "I didn't do it, I tell you! He was lying there like that when I came in—that's all I know about it. I was scared and trying to get away without being noticed, when you grabbed me. You've *got* to believe me—no matter how my being here looks to you!"

"What *were* you doing here?" Wentworth's eyes probed his.

"I came to argue with him. I wanted to try to talk him into withdrawing his charge against Mabel Rice," the clerk admitted. "The door was open so I came in—and that's the way I found him. I swear to God, I didn't do it! You heard me threaten him, but I was excited then. All I wanted was to get him to free Mabel. We're going to be married. You know how I felt—you'd have come here yourself if she were your girl. Let me get out of here, and I'll do anything you say to help you clear her, Mr.

Wentworth," he pleaded. "If they arrest me for this murder, she will have nobody to fight for her."

Wentworth was kneeling beside the disfigured corpse, but there was little it could tell him. The flesh was still warm, although the blood had stopped flowing. Norton might have been killed at any time during the past ten or twenty minutes—might have had that slender dagger driven into his heart the moment he put down the telephone after his frantic plea for help. Except for his presence there in the house, there was nothing to connect young York with the crime....

"You're in a bad spot," Wentworth told him soberly, "and I'm taking chances with the law myself if I let you go. But I'm going to gamble on it. I want your address, and then I want you to go home and stay there until you hear from me."

Phil York was almost hysterical in his profuse thanks. With repeated assurances of his good faith and eagerness to help, he edged his way to the door and fled from the house as if it were plague-stricken.

AS SOON as he was gone, Wentworth went to the telephone to call Kirkpatrick and report this latest development.

"Another!" the commissioner groaned, the moment he had heard the news. "That makes five deaths we can charge up to the Silencer today, Dick. Two more suicides have been reported—Mary Hatfield and Clement Norelius. No disfigurations, but one of those damned Silencer cards was on Norelius' desk. You know what that means—Norelius was a close friend of the mayor."

Wentworth did know what that meant, and his sympathy

went out to Stanley Kirkpatrick in this latest trouble that had come upon him. But again the diabolical power of this criminal, who called himself the Silencer, slapped at him like a direct challenge and sent the red blood throbbing through his veins.

Mary Hatfield, a wealthy young society woman; Clement Norelius, millionaire politician whose counsel reputedly had been of great weight in shaping the policies of the municipal administration... nobody seemed too powerful, too secure, for this creature. Like a great octopus of crime, his tentacles wormed their way into every level of society and brought death to his helpless victims—a murderous monster whom only the Spider could ever hope to exterminate!

CHAPTER 5
HORROR'S WAKE

OWEN GLEASON had proved of little value as a lead to the Silencer, Wentworth considered, but there still remained Sam Latshaw—the hunted murderer who roamed free to prey upon the city although the entire police force was on the lookout for him. Undoubtedly, Latshaw was well covered, hidden away securely in the rat warrens of the underworld—and the only way to locate him was to go down into the underworld and ferret him out of his hole.

Richard Wentworth would get no further in that attempt than the best of Kirkpatrick's men—but it was for just such purposes as this that Blinky McQuade had come into being, been conceived in Wentworth's mind. For this shambling, slovenly East Side denizen was no ordinary man born of woman; he had been created so that Wentworth would have access to underworld resorts which he could not hope to enter in his own guise, resorts where even the Spider could not make an appearance.

Since the day, months before, when Blinky McQuade had rented a slattern room in a tenement on Holian Alley, the underworld had become accustomed to his shambling, furtive coming and going. Accepted first as a mere hanger-on to the fringe of crime, the reputation of the ex-safe-blower had grown until his associates knew that, even though he had been nearly blinded by a premature explosion, the accident had sharpened his faculties, trained his fingers, until he had become an expert cracksman.

Locating Sam Latshaw was a task for Blinky McQuade, and a few minutes later Wentworth was on his way to that maze of dingy tenement-lined streets that lies east of the Bowery. A block from Holian Alley, he dismissed his cab and went the rest of the way on foot, to turn in at Number One, a squalid, filth-littered doorway. He walked up to a room on the second floor… and in the next few minutes Richard Wentworth disappeared.

Kneeling upon the big bed, which was the most imposing article of furniture the place boasted, he pressed his fingers against a panel in its massive head. The panel opened outward to reveal, in the recess behind it, a complete makeup kit spread out before a lighted mirror.

Quickly, he went to work, and, when he was finished, the creature who climbed off the bed was tousle-haired, taut-faced, wizened, his weak eyes blinking out through hooded glasses perched on a strongly arched nose. A seedy-looking suit of clothes and a none too clean shirt, shoes that had seen better days—and, when Blinky McQuade shuffled out of the room and locked the door behind him, not even Wentworth's closest friends would have recognized in this disreputable individual the immaculate clubman and amateur criminologist they knew.

It was dark in "Holy Alley" when Blinky came out into the street, but those hooded glasses in no way handicapped his vision. In fact, the lenses beneath the hoods were long-distance magnifiers that enabled him to see farther and more clearly than anyone supposed.

Keenly, his glance darted up and down the street, as he hesitated momentarily in the doorway. Up and down, and across the way—and there, on the near-by corner, he picked out the figure of Phil York, trying to look inconspicuous as he crowded against a doorway and kept his eyes fastened on the house into which Richard Wentworth had disappeared. Instead of going home, as he had promised, the bank clerk had trailed him to the alley, and now was waiting there to follow him!

Wentworth wondered about that as he made his way through the odorous, congested streets. Had he been mistaken in his judgment of York? Was it possible that the clerk had killed Norton—that he was one of the Silencer's men? Had Norton been right, and was Mabel Rice also a cog in the criminal organization?

The dimly lit entrance to a basement Chinese laundry put an end to those disquieting thoughts. Blinky plodded down the steps and shuffled across the store to a curtain at one side—through that and into a dim hallway that led to another flight of steps. He passed the perch where China Sam sat beside a metal-sheathed door.

THE BLAND-FACED Eurasian bowed, when he recognized his visitor. One of his hands slipped out of a capacious silken sleeve and touched a button beside his perch, and the door slid open soundlessly. With a grunt of acknowledgment, Blinky shuffled into the combination bar, opium joint and lounging-room. A dozen or more hard-looking customers lined the counter or sat arguing at the tables. Over a glass of whisky, he glanced from one to another—until he spied a weasel-like creature sitting by himself in one of the wall booths.

It was Gabby Feldman—an encyclopedia of underworld information which could be read, at a price.

"Been lookin' for you, Gabby," Blinky said softly as he dropped onto the bench across the table from the stool-pigeon. "Have yerself a drink." And then, when Feldman's whisky had been set before him, "Got somethin' I want you to do for me, Gabby—I wanna locate Sam Latshaw. Gotta see him—in a hurry, too… Oh, yeah, I know—you ain't got any idea where he is," he deprecated when Feldman started to protest. "But I *gotta* find him, see? I got hold o' somethin' he ought to know."

Blinky reached for his chaser, and, when he set the glass back on the table, there was a folded ten-dollar bill beneath it. Gabby s eyes gleamed hungrily, but he shook his head dolefully.

"If I knew where he should be, why wouldn't I tell you? he mourned. "All the police are looking for Sam." Blinky lifted the chaser glass half an inch and thrust another folded pad of green beneath it.

"Twenty—and not a damned cent more!" he spat. "If you don't want it, I'll find plenty others ready to take it."

But Feldman was already pushing the glass aside and palming the bills. His shifty eyes darted around the poorly lit room, and he hunched farther over the table.

"I can't guarantee this, understand," he wheezed, "I don't know for sure. But, from what I hear, I think you can probably find him in the Redemption Mission, over on the Bowery. Maybe John Hobey'll know where he is. That's all I c'n do for you, Blinky."

It was sufficient. Latshaw would be at the mission. If Gabby Feldman had not known where to locate him, he would have gone out and not come back until he had the information, rather than let those twenty dollars slip through his fingers. That was what Wentworth told himself as he walked to the Bowery and located the Redemption Mission.

But when he shuffled into the meeting-room, Latshaw was not there.

The evening service evidently was over, yet a score of human derelicts still lounged on the benches—down-and-outers with whom Latshaw would have scorned to associate. Not a criminal worth his salt was among them. As Blinky stood eyeing them, wondering why Feldman had given him such a wild steer, he noticed a florid-faced man with a mop of bushy red hair coming toward him with a smile of welcome and out-stretched hand.

"Good evening, brother," he greeted cordially, as he pumped Blinky's hand. From his black garb and reversed collar, Wentworth knew that this must be John Hobey, the mission manager. "Your face is unfamiliar—but we are always glad to welcome strangers," Hobey was booming. "You are late for the regular service, but if there is any way in which I can be of help, you need only mention it. Perhaps—" he tilted his head and tried to look into Blinky's eyes—"you have some trouble with which you need help—some problem on which you need advice?"

" 'Tain't exactly a problem," Blinky seized his opportunity. "I'm tryin' to locate a pal o' mine—Sam Latshaw." He watched Hobey's face, but there was no change in the set smile that wreathed it from ear to ear. "Heard he was spendin' quite a bit o' time down here with you."

Now the smile slowly faded, and Hobey shook his head regretfully.

"He used to visit us very frequently," he admitted; "but that was before he—er—got into trouble. Since the police have been asking about him, he hasn't been here. No, I haven't seen anything of Latshaw for quite a number of days. Were you—er—associated with him, Mr.—"

"McQuade—Blinky McQuade," Wentworth supplied. "Yeah, I was 'sociated with him, but I ain't seen him lately, neither."

Convinced that there was no information to be gained from

John Hobey, he was backing toward the door. But now the professional smile was again in place on the reformer's face. He clapped his arm around McQuade's shoulders and urged him to stay, offered him hot coffee and a bed for the night—used every bit of cordiality to detain him.

At last, Wentworth managed to get away and shuffled out onto the Bowery, but not before he had drunk a cup of John Hobey's coffee and munched one of his rolls. This lead had been as fruitless as the Gleason one, he told himself, as he turned eastward and trudged back to Holian Alley. Sam Latshaw was hiding out somewhere in this underworld catacombs, but certainly the Redemption Mission was no place to look for him.

It meant that Gabby Feldman would have some tall explaining to do the next time he bumped into Blinky McQuade. Obviously, the stool-pigeon had swindled him—had deliberately sent him on a fool's errand. But why? Because he was covering up Sam Latshaw? Because he, like Latshaw, was numbered in the criminal legion of the Silencer?

Perhaps Gabby Feldman was the very lead he had been seeking! Perhaps the squealer could be forced to divulge his connection with the Silencer. Grimly, Wentworth changed his course and headed back to China Sam's—only to stop in mid-stride, listening with amazed, incredulous ears.

The very ground was shaking under him! That terrific rumble was like an avalanche—an earthquake!

WENTWORTH HAD all the native New Yorker's familiarity with underground noises, mere contempt for muffled explosions that meant nothing more than subway blasting—but this was different, vastly different. Something about it sent a chill creeping down his spine. There had been no explosion—just that ground-shaking rumble, as if the city's foundations were coming down in ruins!

For a moment after that breath-taking crash, there was silence… and then voices seemed to let loose on every side—

The cries of mangled victims, trapped in the collapsed tenements, were still ringing in Wentworth's ears.

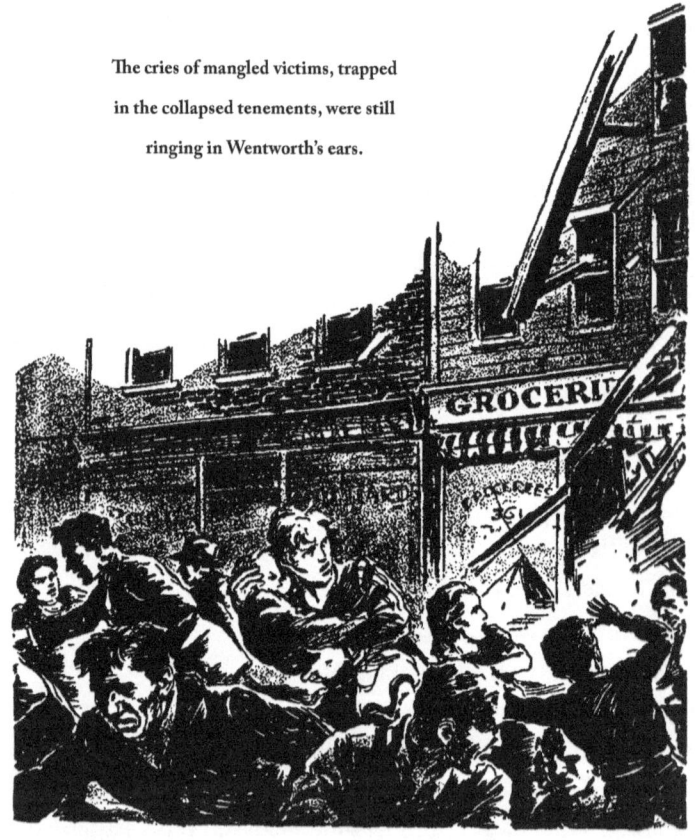

screams of terror, shouts of alarm. Out of tenement doorways, men and women were pouring, to stand, confused and questioning, in the street.

But Wentworth had already seen people running on the avenue, and now he was sprinting after them. Already the avenue was crowded, and, within two blocks, the street was packed with milling humanity—helpless creatures who could only gape and gasp, drowning with their cries the agonized screams that reverberated from the cliff-like tenement fronts.

The crowd was thickest around a spot where that line of grimy fronts was broken—where a gap in the solid wall stood out like a missing tooth. Some of these tenements, Wentworth knew, had been empty so long that their discouraged owners had torn them down rather than attempt to renovate and rebuild them. But, when he wormed his way through the crowd, he saw with a twinge of horror that this was only half of the explanation.

One of those tenements had been torn down… but the one beside it had just collapsed. It had slipped, a mass of disintegrating ruins, into the empty lot where its neighbor had stood! A six-story building, housing twenty-four or more families, it had given way, without warning and carried dozens of its tenants down to their deaths, burying other dozens beneath tons of debris!

The dust of that frightful collapse still hung over the street like a pall, muffling the groans and screams that welled up from the shambles beneath it. Women were shrieking hysterically, children wailing in terror, calling piteously for lost parents, men moaning in agony as they fought to tear their crushed limbs from under timbers that pinned them down helplessly—all these blended in a symphony of suffering that stabbed at Wentworth's heart.

Death was holding high carnival in that tangled mass of ruins, suffocating, choking, grinding the life out of its trapped victims, while their friends and neighbors stood by, too dazed and horrified to go to their rescue! In that dust-shrouded jumble of wreckage, bloody heads were protruding, flailing arms and legs poking up grotesquely, maimed victims crawling on hands and knees—only to give up the hopeless struggle and fall back into the deathtraps surrounding them on every side.

A few of the more hardy onlookers were making ineffectual attempts to be of some help, but it wasn't until Blinky McQuade leaped into the constantly shifting mass of ruins that the crowd came to its senses.

"You men!" he shouted. "Get to work on these timbers! A dozen people are pinned down under them! Hurry up!"

Already, his shoulder was under a heavy beam, straining to lift it, while a young fellow, who had answered his call, wedged his way beneath it and dragged out an old woman whose legs seemed broken. From all sides, the screams and moans sobbed into Wentworth's ears, spurring him on to greater effort. Time and again, he lost his unstable footing, as the shifting mass of wreckage gave way beneath him. He was almost trapped beneath a new shower of bricks and plaster. But, gradually, he organized the rescue squads, set the men to digging and burrowing with some semblance of order, the women to taking care of the rescued victims until the ambulances arrived to attend them.

At last, the cries of the trapped sufferers subsided, and only silence—the ghastly silence of the tomb—came from the ruins. Blinky straightened his aching back and rubbed a tattered shirt sleeve across his perspiring face—when again the ground beneath him trembled!

That was no shifting of the wreckage. It was the very ground beneath the wreckage that was quaking as a deafening rumble and ear-splitting crash blotted out all other sounds!

WITH THE first tremor, Blinky's eyes had flashed, fearfully, to the building beside him. It was still intact—but across the street another tenement was coming apart like a house built of children's blocks! Half of it was already in ruins, the rest falling away, sliding downward, taking with it a crazy mass of furniture and screaming victims trapped in their beds!

Again, a shrouding cloud of blinding dust rose mercifully to blot out the horrors beneath it, the night air rent by screams of agony. As Blinky stood there, gazing at the spot where, a moment before, a crowded tenement had been standing, he realized that these horrible cataclysms were no accidents! They had been diabolically planned!

Just before that building had disintegrated he had heard the muffled *boom*, felt the slight tremor of an explosion. That tenement had been undermined, the deathtrap already prepared so that it might be sprung at any moment. Both buildings had been standing there, waiting for Death to set off the charge that would mean destruction!

Now the narrow street was swarming with panic-stricken people, as the terrified tenants poured out of every other building on the block, expecting their homes to collapse around their ears at any moment. Shrieking fire apparatus, sirening police cars, clanging ambulances, converged on the scene and added to the mêlée, glutting the street from curb to curb. All of the swarming East Side seemed to be packed into that death-smitten block—which, Blinky realized, was just what the devil, who had planned this horror, wanted!

This merciless slaughter had been staged to center attention on this block and remove scrutiny from somewhere else....

But from where? There were no banks or wealthy stores in this desolate neighborhood, nothing worth robbing. And then Wentworth saw his mistake, realized the stake for which these innocent lives had been ruthlessly sacrificed.

Limping his way out of the tangled ruins, he shouldered a path through the densely packed crowd. All the way to the distant corner, that street swarmed with people, but at last he was free of them. He went across the avenue and into a block that was deserted as if its congested buildings were uninhabited. At a dog-trot he ran on toward the river, his eyes scanning the empty streets, now lined with warehouses instead of tenements. Not a soul was to be seen in these silent blocks. Not a—

And then suddenly he darted across the street, to where a groaning man on his knees was clutching a water hydrant, desperately trying to get back onto his feet!

Half-erect, the fellow staggered—and then all the strength seemed to go out of him as he wilted and collapsed. Wentworth reached his side just in time to catch and ease him to the sidewalk. Blood was streaming from a ghastly wound in his head, soaking one leg of his trousers as it poured from another in his thigh. His eyes were already glazed, but he was making a frantic effort to speak.

"Yukon Furs," Wentworth made out the words as he put his ear close to the barely moving lips. "Watchman there… robbery."

For a moment, the filming eyes closed, and the gasping voice was still. Wentworth slipped a hand beneath the man's coat, felt for the faintly beating heart. Desperation seemed to give the watchman new strength.

"We had a double guard tonight—'nother man besides myself. Very valuable shipment of furs come in today," he rushed on as if he feared that every word would be his last. "Gang of thieves got in the warehouse. Other watchman was one of them—he let them in. They almost killed me… left me for dead. But I got out the side door, just as they drove away. I…."

Red bubbles crimsoned the dying man's lips, and drowned the words in his throat. Gently, Wentworth eased him to the pavement. This, as he had feared, was the answer to those collapsing buildings—a cold-blooded plot to loot a richly stocked fur warehouse. Dozens of lives sacrificed so that these thieves could work without interruption!

Grim-faced, Blinky McQuade walked further into the fur district, and, as he went, he realized that the robbery of the Yukon Furs' warehouse was only part of the carefully staged raid. Now, burglar alarms were clamoring all around him, dinning into the night calls for help that would not be answered until long after the thieves, who had set them off, were gone. Twice, a heavily loaded truck careened past him, and once he threw himself into the shelter of a doorway just in time to miss a burst of tommy-gun lead that hailed at him from a passing car.

System was the keynote of this raid. While gangs of thieves looted the warehouse, cars full of killers patrolled the entire neighborhood to shoot down anyone who might straggle into it. Twice more, Wentworth discovered the bodies of murdered watchmen—and before he turned back to Holian Alley he was convinced that the entire fur district had been looted. Dozens of warehouses must have been stripped of their contents at the very height of their season, a time when they were loaded to capacity.

The thoroughness and perfect timing of that coup pointed unmistakably to the Silencer. Human suffering meant nothing to that devil, human lives even less. The agonized cries of those mangled victims, trapped in the collapsed tenements, were still ringing in Wentworth's ears, the scenes of grisly horror still fresh in his mind's eye. As he plodded back to Holian Alley, he was burning with rage.

The inhuman monster would pay for this night's carnage, he swore grimly—would pay for each of those brutally snuffed-out lives, for all of the agony he had mercilessly decreed….

NUMBER ONE Holian Alley was an ideal residence for Blinky McQuade and his fellow tenants, for more than one reason. Not only was it buried in one of the most chopped-up and congested districts of the slums, but it was located at the point of a triangle where "Holy Alley" and Pallin Place intersected and formed a sharp V. The rear of the house on the Pallin Place arm of the V looked out on a dark little court that also served as a backyard for its Holian Alley neighbor—circumstance that greatly facilitated the hasty comings and going of the residents of both buildings.

Now, instead of turning in at the dirty, paint-peeled door of Number One, Blinky McQuade shuffled up Pallin Place and through the hallway of that building to the courtyard at its rear. Coming out into the little stone-flagged patch, he glanced upward—and saw that the hunch which had prompted this indirect approach was well founded.

Hanging from the window of the Pallin Place apartment that almost touched the window of his own room was a single white towel—warning from the girl who lived there that someone was waiting for him behind his locked door!

Warily, Blinky picked his way across the court and into the opposite hallway, up the dank, evil-smelling stairs to the second floor. Cautiously, he thrust his key into the old-fashioned lock, turned it—and suddenly flung the door inward as he dived to the floor with arms outstretched in a football tackle.

One of his clutching hands closed around a man's leg, and, in the next moment, the fellow thudded to the floor. Breath went out of him with a surprised gasp. But that jarring thud incapacitated him for only an instant—then he became a bundle of springs. Viciously, he tore himself out of Blinky's grip and bounded back against the wall, a savage curse ripping from his lips.

The only light in that stygian arena was a patch of gray that trickled in through the murky window pane—but its feeble glow was sufficient to gleam momentarily on the blade of a knife. Blinky hurled himself to one side, as the razor-sharp blade swept down at him and sliced through his sleeve. Then he was in on top of the fellow's knife-arm before he could raise it for another swipe, pinning it against his body and smashing his head back with a butt under the chin.

Together, they pitched to the floor, rolling over and over, while Blinky's steely fingers fastened on the other's knife-wrist and sank deep into its tendons. Frenziedly, the fellow fought—with fist and feet, knees and head, snapping, gnashing teeth. But Blinky had drawn his own head down deep within the protection of his shoulders, and his fingers were busy with that knife-wrist… turning it….

Suddenly the fellow screamed thinly and tried to squirm away from his own hand, that held the terrible knife. But it followed him inexorably, biting into his side, jabbing deeper.

"Stop it!" he gasped frantically. "For God's sake—stop before you drive it through my guts! Ugh-h—"

Now he was trying to drop the knife, to release his fingers from the hilt—but Blinky's grip had slipped down over his hand and would not relinquish its hold. The point went deeper. Warm blood oozed out over Blinky's hand—and then the fellow went limp.

"You're killing me!" brokenly. "You're gonna murder me! Geez—gimme a chance! I'll do anything you say! Take that damned knife out of my belly!"

With his free hand, Blinky fished in his pocket for a packet of matches, tore one loose and struck it—to leap erect and touch it to the gas-jet before his would-be murderer knew what was happening.

59

Knife in hand, Blinky stood over him, looking down into the terrified face of Sam Latshaw, the killer the entire police force was hunting!

"So it's you, Latshaw," Wentworth stood ready as the killer got to his feet and cringed back against the wall. "I've been wantin' to see you. Now, you're gonna answer some questions fast. You're working with the Silencer. All right—who is he?"

"I don't know, McQuade—so help me God!" Latshaw swore. "I get my orders over the telephone-and do what I'm told. I can't help myself. He knows all about me. If I try to double-cross him, he'll turn me over to the police. I seen what happened to other smart guys who tried to put somethin' over on him—"

He slumped on the bed, all the fight apparently gone out of him. For an instant, his ratty eyes flashed up at Blinky's face, read the disbelief there.

"I'm not the only one—there's plenty of others he's got the screws on," he protested. "Plenty o' wanted guys thought they were covered safe—until this guy calls up an' gives them their orders. You read what happened to Whitey Meehan—how the cops found his body in a trunk? That was because he told that voice on the phone to go to hell…."

Latshaw's left hand moved toward his inside coat pocket, as he spoke. His eyes never left Blinky's hooded glasses as his fumbling fingers crinkled the papers in that pocket—then suddenly whipped out a shoulder-holstered automatic.

The trick was almost perfect. But Latshaw could not control that almost imperceptible tightening of the muscles which heralds sudden action. Blinky's alert eyes caught the slight tensing of the body—and the moment that gun appeared, his fist lashed out in a back-hand blow that sent the weapon spinning across the room.

With an oath, Latshaw was off the bed, diving after the gun. Evil, gloating sounds chuckled from his throat, as his fingers closed on it. He whirled in a killer's crouch. But before he could pull the trigger, a streak of light lanced across the room. Stark amazement fairly popped the eyes out of his head. The automatic dropped from his nerveless fingers. He crumpled and fell, face forward, on the floor, the thrown knife embedded in his throat.

"Once more I owe my life to you, mighty warrior," Wentworth whispered his thanks to the absent Ram Singh, his faithful Sikh body servant, who had spent long hours teaching him to throw a knife as accurately as a bullet.

WITHOUT ANOTHER glance at the corpse of the man who had come there to murder him, Blinky turned out the light and peered down for a moment into the murk of the courtyard. Not a sound from there. Nor was there any evidence of activity in the hall. The residents of Holian Alley were not an inquisitive breed; it would take more than a rough-and-tumble fight to bring them investigating.

With a nod of satisfaction, he stepped out into the hall and locked the door behind him. Ten minutes' walk brought him to a boarded-up factory. An alley ran beside it to a row of sheet-iron garages at its rear, and, from one of these, he drove an inconspicuous-looking little car that could perform unsuspected wonders should the emergency arrive. He drove it back to Holian Alley to take Sam Latshaw on his last ride.

Halfway across town, the car stopped before a small Italian restaurant that was closed for the night. From the seat beside him, Blinky lifted the corpse of Sam Latshaw and carried it to the doorway, propping it up in a sitting position against the window. For a moment, he bent over it, pressed the bottom of a cigarette lighter to the killer's forehead—and, when he turned back to the car, a crimson spider was stamped indelibly on the white skin.

In the morning the police would marvel at finding the body of Sam Latshaw in the doorway of the little restaurant that had belonged to Tony Magnozzi, the man for whose murder Latshaw was sought—and the Silencer would know that his challenge had been accepted—that the Spider was on his trail!

CHAPTER 6
THE LISTENERS

RICHARD WENTWORTH slept the sleep of exhaustion that night. It seemed that his head had hardly touched the pillow, when the ringing of the telephone beside his bed awoke him. Immediately, he was alert, faculties fully organized. That call must be important, or old Jenkyns, his valet, would not have put it through from the switchboard that connected with each room in the four-story building.

Swiftly, into his mind flashed recollection of the past night's events, and he was fully prepared to hear the voice of the Silencer when he picked up the receiver.

Instead, it was Nita van Sloan, agitated, trembling.

"It's happened again, Dick—another suicide!" she exclaimed. "Roy Pelton—Marjorie's husband! He shot himself a little while ago. I'm at their place now. Marjorie was hysterical when I arrived, and the doctor gave her an opiate. Before she went to sleep, she said enough to make me certain that Roy was blackmailed. I can tell you more when she wakes up. But I *know* it was the Silencer!"

Marjorie Pelton—one of Nita's college chums and closest friends! Wentworth knew the affection each held for the other, and his heart went out to Nita. But blackmail? That seemed impossible in connection with Roy Pelton, a fine, clean-cut, upstanding young fellow, the treasurer and one of the trustees of an airplane concern. The last man in the world one would suspect of suicide....

"Isn't anyone safe from that monster?" Nita echoed his own thoughts. "He terrifies me, Dick—makes me feel that you or I may be next!"

"Forget it, Nita!" Wentworth's tone was sharp, as he heard her tremor. "I'll come right over there to pick you up and take you down to Kirk. He'll want to hear about this."

Kirkpatrick did want to hear about Roy Pelton's death—a lot more than was in Nita's power to tell. The commissioner's eyes were heavy, tired, as if he had spent a sleepless night; even the gardenia in his buttonhole looked wilted and discouraged. Wearily, he turned from fruitlessly cross-examining Nita, and waved toward a sheaf of reports on his desk.

"He operates all over the city," he muttered dourly, "and yet there is never a tangible clue. Everything is too carefully planned, organized. Last night, ten warehouses in the fur district were robbed. The raid was timed to perfection and struck when the warehouses were bulging with furs. Yukon Furs had just taken in a shipment worth close to a quarter million. More than half was to be shipped out again today. But last night the place was looted from cellar to roof." He frowned.

"It's just as if these thieves know exactly what night to strike, Dick—as if they were directed by the furriers, themselves. That's the outstanding feature of this crime wave. Every job seems to be based on inside information that the victims, alone, could have possessed. It sounds like wire-tappers—but it would take hundreds of them to conduct a campaign of such magnitude!"

Wire-tappers... Wentworth's thoughts were leaping ahead of the commissioner. Ordinary wiretapping, he admitted, seemed impossible on a scale so wide. That was just what Arthur Morrell had pointed out....

Suddenly, into his mind flashed the dying words of the telephone company general manager. Something about an employee who had been discharged from the laboratory for experimenting with wire-tapping. When Morrell had been on the verge of naming that employee, his mouth was stopped with a bullet....

WHILE NITA went to comfort Marjorie Pelton and to learn what more she could of Roy's suicide, Wentworth took a cab to the main office of the telephone company. Bitterly, he cursed himself for having overlooked that obvious lead. Arthur Morrell's life had been snuffed out to conceal the name of that unknown experimenter—perhaps to block a direct lead to the Silencer! Certainly, the fellow ought to have been investigated.

Warner Keller was seated at the desk that had been Morrell's, when Wentworth was ushered into the office. His heavy-featured face already showed the strain of his responsibilities. Never an amiable man, the scowl that was his usual expression gave his face a Satanic cast—an impression enhanced by the curling hair which turned upward like horns above his temples.

"You have no official standing, Wentworth," he snapped, as soon as he heard the purpose of the interview. "It's bad enough having the police prowling all over the place and asking stupid questions. If we open our files to every would-be detective, we might as well close up shop and quit trying to do any business."

"I don't want to prowl through your files," Wentworth patiently assured him. "All I want is the name of the laboratory man who was fired for his wire-tapping experiments—the man whose name was on Morrell's lips when he was shot down from that doorway—"

Keller almost leaped out of his chair, as he flashed a glance to the door which opened into what had been his old office. Now the door was half-ajar, Vincent Crosby, his secretary, standing hesitantly on the threshold with several papers in his hand. Crosby opened his mouth, tried to speak, but Keller cut him short.

"Not now—I'm busy!" he fairly shouted. "Damn it, Crosby—I've told you to knock before you come in here!" Scowling bleakly, he turned back to Wentworth, the dark eyes, beneath his bushy brows, wary and suspicious. "I don't know anything about any wire-tapping experiments," he snapped. "If I did, it would be contrary to company policy to tell you about it!"

65

"Then you refuse to coöperate?" Wentworth rose and stood beside the desk. "With, or without, your aid, I'll locate this man, Keller. In doing it, I may discover the reason for your opposition."

Perhaps it was the implied threat, perhaps the grim expression on Wentworth's tight-lipped face. Suddenly, Keller yielded. With a forced smile, he leaned back in his chair and rang for Crosby.

"Maybe I've been a bit out of order, Wentworth," he admitted. "My nerves aren't what they might be—after what happened yesterday. I'll have Crosby take you down to the laboratory. The manager should be able to locate your man. If there's anything else I can do to help apprehend the hound who killed poor old Morrell, just let me know."

That sudden about-face wasn't natural, nor convincing. Something was behind it, and Wentworth groped for the answer. But Crosby was there at his side, waiting to lead the way to the experimental laboratory and introduce him to the manager.

"We have lost four men during the past year," the laboratory chief checked up. "Three left to take other positions. All are working here in New York. The other—let me see, his name was Herman Steckel, a man about fifty—I never did know why he was let out. We were talking about him the other day. I heard that he went back to his home in Missouri."

Crosby suggested that the personnel bureau would have the address on file. He stayed with Wentworth until they ascertained that Herman Steckel's home town was Adalia, a town on the outskirts of Kansas City.

THERE WAS a noon plane to Kansas City, Wentworth checked up. He barely made it. From Kansas City, a taxi drove him to Adalia—to the old farmhouse just outside of town that was Herman Steckel's home. But the inventor wasn't there.

"He went to New York early in the week." The elderly woman, who introduced herself as his wife, shook her head regretfully and urged Wentworth to come inside.

There were two other members of the family, a daughter in her early twenties and a husky son a few years older. All three were very willing to talk—and quickly corroborated Wentworth's suspicions. "Yes, Daddy kept working on his invention, after he came back from New York," the girl told him. "I never saw what it looked like—he's awfully secret about his work—but I know it's some sort of thingamajig for listening on the telephone without using a receiver. He perfected it about a month after he came home."

"That was when he went back to New York and sold it." The older woman nodded. "Since then, he hasn't had to work at all—every month his check comes in the mail. But now he thinks it isn't large enough. He says the people who bought his invention are making a fortune with it, and he wants more money. That's why he is in New York now."

Making a fortune? If Wentworth's hunch was right, and it was Herman Steckel's invention that was the basis of the Silencer's criminal campaign, the possibilities of the thing were stupendous—appalling! Millions of dollars of blackmail toll, evil power unlimited, a criminal organization such as the world had never seen—all these might lie in the palm of that clutching hand!

And Herman Steckel, who had made these things possible, could lead the way to the man who was forging them on a shuddering anvil of human suffering and death....

"What is his address in New York?" Wentworth tried to keep the eagerness out of his voice. "I want to talk to him about his invention, but unless I can see him at once, it will be too late."

All three of the Steckels rose to that bait, but none of them knew where the inventor could be located. They had not heard from him since he left—supposed he was at some hotel, but had no idea which. If only Mr. Wentworth could wait?

"If you must go right back, maybe Mr. Keller could tell you where he is staying," the daughter finally suggested. "He's the man who sends Daddy the checks. I don't know his first name, but I think he's somebody important in the telephone company."

Warner Keller! Wentworth recalled his instinctive distrust of the man, the peculiar circumstances of Arthur Morrell's death. Morrell had been killed from the doorway of Keller's office. He might easily have been killed by Keller. But that left no explanation of the man Vincent Crosby had seen running across the office—unless the fellow was one of Keller's killers or the Silencer's bloody assistants....

That very morning Keller had denied any knowledge of Herman Steckel, the man to whom his checks were going regularly! A damning circumstance, that—and one Keller would have a tough time explaining. Recollection of his surliness and sudden baffling change of attitude, added fuel to Wentworth's kindling suspicions. He knew that he must get back to New York at the earliest possible moment!

But when he returned to Kansas City, he found that there was no east-bound plane leaving that night—none until the next morning. Grounded there, a thousand miles from New York, he was helpless.

If only there were some way of contacting Kirkpatrick or Nita—but he did not dare even to use the telephone or telegraph. He had no way of knowing the extent of the Silencer's wire-tapping organization. To telephone Kirkpatrick might be to tip off Keller and give him the chance to make a get-away before the police could nab him….

No, this was no job to be delegated to others. It was a grim task for the Spider, alone!

CHAPTER 7
REIGN OF TERROR

MARJORIE PELTON was just awakening from her drugged sleep when Nita van Sloan returned to the stricken household. Tearfully, the young widow clung to her, pouring out the hysterical account of her tragedy.

"Everything was going to be all right," she sobbed. "Every dollar would have been paid back, and nobody ever would have known. We had worried so, but it was all coming out all right. Then, just at the last moment, everything went to pieces! Roy was murdered, Nita! He was forced to kill himself by an inhuman devil—a monster who might just as well have fired that very bullet into his head!"

Gradually, Nita quieted her and drew out the story more fully.

"It all started a year ago," Marjorie said. "Roy's father's business was in very bad shape. His credit was exhausted, and he had to have money or be forced into bankruptcy. Not that the business wasn't a good investment. It was—it was worth every dollar that had been put into it and a great deal more. In fact, it was so good that Mr. Pelton's competitors were trying to force him out of it and take it away from him." She wiped her eyes.

"That would have broken the old gentleman's heart and killed him. Roy knew that, and worried over it until he was sick. Then he solved the thing in his own way. He didn't tell me until after he had done it—and then it was too late to do anything but hope that it would come out all right.

"You know that Roy was treasurer of his company, Nita. Well, he borrowed a hundred thousand dollars of the company money and loaned it to his father—borrowed it without letting the rest of the directors know anything about it. I know that sounds terrible, but it really wasn't. The money was perfectly safe, and there was no question about being able to pay it back. Roy just had to keep the shortage concealed until he could replace it.

"His father had repaid half the money and just completed arrangements to have the other half repaid by a man who was going into his business with him. Last night, he telephoned Roy and told him that the money would be in the bank by the end of the week. That was a terrible load off our shoulders. We promised each other we'd have a party Saturday night to celebrate, just the two of us—the only ones who knew.

"But someone else knew, Nita! He telephoned early this morning, before we were up. *He demanded that Roy pay him another hundred thousand dollars to keep silent!* When Roy said he didn't have that much money and couldn't possibly raise it, the man on the wire told him to get it out of the company funds the way he had done for his father. He threatened to expose that loan to the other directors, unless Roy promised to do as he was told.

" 'I'm at the mercy of a blood-sucking blackmailer,' Roy whispered to me when he told me what that call was about. 'How in God's name he learned what he knows I can't understand—but he does know, and he'll make a common thief of me. He'll force me to loot the company treasury, and then he'll ruin my father, as well. I can't let him do that, Marjorie.' "

"He held me tight and kissed me, and then, before I could say a word, he went into the next room and closed the door— and I heard the shot!" she finished with a burst of tears. "Oh, how could anyone be so inhuman? How could anyone do such a thing?" Her eyes stared widely.

But Nita had seen too much of the seamy side of life to marvel at the limits to which some men will go to get their hands on easy money. What she wanted to know was how this blackmailer had learned of Roy Pelton's shortage.

"Only Roy and his father and you knew about this unauthorized loan?" she questioned. "You're sure about that, Marjorie?"

"Positively," the young widow affirmed. "Even the man who

71

is paying Mr. Pelton the rest of the money doesn't know how it is to be used. All he knows is that he is investing in Mr. Pelton's business."

"There wasn't anyone here who might have overheard that telephone conversation last night? Nobody who might have overheard it on Mr. Pelton's end of the wire?"

"No," Marjorie was positive. "We were alone here—and I remember Roy thought of that, too. He questioned his father

about it, and Mr. Pelton said that he was alone in a booth at his club."

And yet that conversation *must* have been overheard—that was the only leak through which the blackmailer could have secured his information. One by one, Nita reviewed the suicides of the past few weeks, and, in each one, blackmail was the only reasonable motive. Again, she heard Lenore Gleason's voice sobbing a plea for help over the wire, "He knows all about Earl—"

73

That "he" was the Silencer—the blackmailer who was prying into people's lives and wielding their innermost secrets, like clubs, over their heads! Secrets which he had filched from their own unsuspecting telephone conversations!

Wire-tapping was at the bottom of this crime wave; all the evidence fitted together so perfectly that she was sure of it. Like an omnipresent eavesdropper, the Silencer, or one of his men, sat listening, preying on the city's telephone conversations and wringing from them a fearful toll in dollars and in human misery!

WITH THAT conviction, a daring plan began to take form in Nita's seething brain. It was full-blown by the time she reached police headquarters and was ushered into Kirkpatrick's office. Silently, the commissioner listened while she outlined her scheme. But before she was finished, his frown had deepened and his head was shaking in weary disapproval.

"I admit that the city is in the hands of a gigantic blackmail ring," he confessed. "I admit that I think you are right in suspecting that they operate by some method of wholesale wire-tapping. More than half of the robberies, hold-ups and suicides during the past six weeks have been the result of information which was extorted from the victims, themselves—information that must have come from their own telephones.

"I admit that, Nita—but we haven't been able to do a thing to combat it. Your plan might work, but it's entirely too dangerous. Once you were suspected—" his eyes narrowed and his hands gripped the arms of his chair until they were white-knuckled—

"we'd find you with half of your face eaten away by the acid hand of the Silencer!"

"But I won't let the Silencer suspect me, Stanley," she said simply. "My plan will work—where those of your police are bound to fail. I'm going to go through with it before this fiend ruins more lives. I'll let you know when it's time for you to take a hand."

With that, she was gone—on her way to a conference with a trusted friend whose cooperation she would need in this plan that must not fail....

EVEN BEFORE Richard Wentworth got back to New York, word of the Silencer's renewed activities met him. While the plane in which he traveled was still hundreds of miles from the metropolis, the voice of one of the news broadcasters reached into the heavens with its sorry tale of rampant and unchecked crime.

"Audacious kidnaping on a wholesale scale was today added to the growing list of unpunished crimes that have been sweeping New York," came from the loudspeaker. "Between nine o'clock this morning and noon, three women, prominent in the city's social life, left their homes and have not been seen since. Mrs. George van Deusen, Mrs. Otis Howells and Mrs. Stanley Bainbridge apparently are the victims of this latest outrage. The husbands of all three have reported to the police receiving taunting telephone warnings which are the only clues to the missing women."

George van Deusen, Otis Howells, Stanley Bainbridge— as Wentworth listened to those names his heart sank. Men of wealth and influence, each of them. Men who had been working with Commissioner Kirkpatrick and the mayor in an attempt to uncover the Silencer. This was his answer to their interference!

Not until the plane landed at the airport, and he had talked with Nita on the telephone, did that nightmare leave Wentworth. Then he hailed a cab and started for the main office of the telephone company to have the showdown with Warner Keller. But when he arrived, the new general manager was not in his office.

"He hasn't been in all afternoon," Vincent Crosby apologized worriedly. "Several people have been looking for him, and I've tried to locate him at his home and his club. He's not in either place, and I don't know where else to inquire. I'll have him call you when he comes in, Mr. Wentworth."

Warily, Wentworth left Keller's office and the building, but there was no attempt to molest him. Nor could he detect any signs of pursuit as he drove uptown to Sutton Place.

"There has been a young lady calling you all day—a Miss Mabel Rice," Jenkyns reported as soon as Wentworth stepped out of the automatic elevator into the lobby of his stronghold. The buzzing of the switchboard echoed the old man's words.

"Mr. Wentworth," the operator's voice came, low and excited, the moment he picked up the receiver, "I have what you want. I've been so afraid I would not be able to reach you in time. Gleason has been talking plenty—last night and this morning. From what I've heard, I'm sure that he's the Silencer—or at least one of the Silencer's chief assistants. There have been lots of men calling up here for orders, and Gleason tells them all to be on hand tonight."

"Where—there at the building?" Wentworth clipped.

"No, it's some place they call 'Dumpy's'—I have the address copied down." She paused for a moment and then read it to him—an address on East Twenty-sixth Street that must be near First Avenue, Wentworth judged. "They go in through the basement—and they're going to be there at eight-thirty," the girl finished. "I am keeping a transcript of all his conversations, but that is the only important thing I have noticed."

Wentworth commended her warmly before he hung up.

Quickly, he changed into an inconspicuous suit and dark topcoat and then taxied to the corner of First Avenue and Twenty-sixth—a drab, down-at-the-heels neighborhood that had not even the lush vitality of the more congested slums further downtown.

The number he sought proved to be a six-story building that was boarded up from top to bottom! Solid planking blanked out the doorway and every window!

From across the street, Wentworth regarded the place dubiously and wondered whether this rendezvous was a decoy, a clever trap, into which he had obligingly stepped. Then he suddenly became alert, stepped back into the shadowy maw of a hallway. A man, apparently shuffling down the street, had ducked into the railed-off areaway in front of the building… and did not reappear.

During the next ten minutes, two others dropped unobtrusively into the patch of darkness beneath the low stoop of the building. Now it was after eight-thirty—nearly a quarter to nine. The meeting must be in progress behind those boarded-up windows.

WENTWORTH WENT down the block and crossed the street. Like the arrivals he had watched, he slouched close to the buildings, then stepped through the unfastened gate and into that pool of blackness. There was a door at the foot of half a dozen stone steps—a door that creaked open when he turned the knob.

The noise of the rusty hinges seemed deafening in the dead quiet, but it attracted no attention. There was not a sound in the building. Even the air that came out of it seemed dead and cold, as if no living thing had breathed it for months. He felt his way into a musty-smelling hall, one hand gripping an automatic while the other plucked a pencil-sized flashlight from his pocket.

Its tiny beam revealed nothing but desolation. Crumbling walls, ceilings that were cracked and hanging down in great chunks like man-made stalactites, rotted floors that sagged and creaked beneath his weight. Room after room, he investigated and found nothing but moldy rubbish and a litter of filth—until the white face of a corpse stared up at him from the floor!

That face was half eaten away—hideously disfigured with the savage imprint of the Silencer!

Gingerly, he reached into the pockets and brought out an empty wallet with an identification card beneath its celluloid window—a card with a snapshot of the dead face and the name and address of Herman Steckel!

Only then did Wentworth notice the limp fingers of the man's right hand. All but the index finger were still half-curled into a loose fist, but that stood off by itself, the tip smudged with the dust that lay thick on the floor. In that dust was a tracing—the wavery, uncertain outline of three letters, *K E L*—

Three letters—and a fading streak as the dying man's failing muscles had relaxed and given up their desperate attempt to leave a record of the name of his murderer!

CHAPTER 8
HELL'S CLEARING HOUSE

WARNER KELLER again—ruthlessly silencing the lips of the inventor who could have betrayed him, and at the same time serving warning on Wentworth to keep away!

"One more death for which Keller will come to an accounting," Wentworth promised the wide-eyed corpse.

From floor to floor, he tramped, through a monotonous succession of musty, long-empty rooms. Nowhere was there the slightest evidence of recent occupancy—until he came back to the basement hallway and bent close to the floor. There, in the dust, his light picked out the faint trace of footsteps that led to a back door. This door was now locked but must recently have been open to permit the escape of those stooges he had seen going into the building.

The Silencer, Keller, Gleason—someone had tricked him neatly, Wentworth realized. Those telephone conversations

Mabel Rice had overheard had been deliberately planted so that they would be relayed back to him.

Gleason's part in the frame-up was undoubted, but Wentworth could not credit the man with the potentialities of the Silencer. He might be one of the master criminal's lieutenants, one of the pawns in the game—but even that, Wentworth realized suddenly, made him dangerous. Obviously, he knew that Mabel Rice had been planted at his switchboard. They knew that she was covering his wire for Wentworth—and that knowledge might already have sealed her doom.

Wentworth slipped out of the basement entrance and walked west until he found a store with a telephone booth. First, he dialed the number of the girl's apartment, but there was no answer. Perhaps she had gone to Phil York's place? Wentworth tried that number, and the result was the same. Either she had gone out for the evening, or already the trap had closed around her....

Gleason would know whether that was so, and this time, Wentworth resolved grimly, the gambler would talk. This time, there would be no advance telephone call to warn him of Wentworth's coming and give him an opportunity to arrange for a reception committee. There would be no announcement until he answered his door and stared into the snout of an automatic.

But when Wentworth arrived at the gambler's apartment house and went up to his floor there was no response to the bell. Nor was there an answer to the telephone from downstairs in the lobby. Gleason was out, just as everyone else seemed to be.

Hopelessly, Wentworth tried Keller's office again. Vincent

Crosby was still at work, anxiously trying to locate his chief—but of Warner Keller there had been no word.

Every lead to the Silencer had been blocked.

Richard Wentworth's effectiveness, it seemed, was gone; but the Silencer must still reckon with Blinky McQuade….

THAT NIGHT came the sensational safe robbery, a supposedly burglar-proof "box" that was cracked without the use of explosives—and when Blinky McQuade shuffled into his old haunts the next morning, more than one sly wink and leer gave him silent recognition and approval. Balmy, ex-pug proprietor of the high-class criminal Bit House, was grinning with relish and pointing out the newspaper account to several of his patrons.

The grin on Balmy's battle-scarred visage widened, and he turned to his bartender.

"On the house," he nodded to the whisky bottle from which Blinky was pouring his drink—Balmy's way of bestowing the accolade for a job neatly turned.

Several dozen customers were in the Bit House that morning, hardened criminals all of them—men who had done their bit in at least one of the country's penal institutions. But they were unusually quiet, almost furtive.

Without being told, Blinky guessed the reason for that caution. A new power had risen in the underworld, a new master who was known only as the Silencer—and fear of his swift discipline had effectively stilled the boldest tongues!

But Balmy was willing to talk. Soon he sidled up to Blinky's side and mumbled a few words that were an invitation to accompany him to the back-room cubbyhole that was his office.

"Somethin's stirrin'?" Blinky's owlish eyes peered out questioningly.

"Lot o' loose talk never gets you nowhere," the ring-scarred veteran philosophized, "except maybe in trouble up to your ears."

"With the Silencer, eh?"

"Better not go mentioning no names," Balmy muttered uneasily. "Lucky thing you come in, though," he quickly regained his enthusiasm. "I was just wonderin' where to pick you up. The party you mentioned can use you. I had a call this mornin'."

"I'm pretty well fixed," McQuade yawned. "Won't be needin' any cash for a while. Maybe in a month or two—"

"Nix on that, Blinky," the Bit House proprietor leaned forward in quick alarm. "You don't wanna go talkin' that way, when this feller sends for you. I'm offerin' you a chance to make some easy dough—big money and everything fixed so that there's no chance of a slip-up. If you ain't got sense enough to grab that—well, I ain't sayin' what might happen, but I wouldn't turn this feller down, not me."

"So that's the way it is?" Blinky nodded understandingly. "Won't do me no harm to listen to his proposition anyway, I s'pose. Where do I go to see him?"

"I'll fix that up for you," Balmy brightened. "Come down again tonight about eight, and I'll let you know."

All afternoon Blinky shuffled from place to place, into dingy back rooms and down into cellars, up rickety tenement stairs and into "club rooms" in old factories and warehouses—wherever the underworld gathered, from the hangouts of cheap sneak-thieves to the resorts that catered only to the aristocracy of crime. And wherever he went it was the same—everywhere, he could feel the influence of the Silencer.

The more Blinky saw, the more he realized that he must not fail, and by the time he kept his appointment at the Bit House his assumed indifference of the morning had vanished. To all appearances, Blinky McQuade was a very much subdued and impressed crook, quite willing to do as he was told when Balmy took him uptown to an office building a stone's throw from Times Square.

A SMARTLY uniformed starter eyed them, as they stepped into the elevator. An alert operator sped them up to the fifteenth floor, and Balmy led the way into a small private office where a well groomed, trim-looking young executive sat at wide, flat-topped mahogany desk. *Interborough Employment Agency,* Blinky had glimpsed the gold lettering on the door, as they entered. Now the clerk had taken an index card out of his desk and was preparing to write a note on it.

"Blinky McQuade," he repeated, and wrote down the name, as Balmy made the introduction. "Now, Mr. McQuade—"

To his amazement, Wentworth found himself being interviewed like an applicant for any everyday job. He began enlarging on Blinky McQuade's experience as a safe-cracker, boasting of his ability—while the interviewer nodded his head and made cryptic notations on the card.

"Very good," he commented at last. "I think we can use you, McQuade. Perhaps something will turn up for you tonight. If there is, our proposition will be explained to you more fully. Now, if you will just wait in here—"

He had opened a side door, and Blinky was ushered into a large general office and seated on one of a number of benches ranged outside a wooden railing. A dozen underworld characters were already lined up. Inside that railing were twenty-odd desks, each with a man busily at work behind it. Most of the workers wore telephone headpieces and seemed to be taking down message after message. The others were equally industriously laboring over stacks of index cards, filing them away in little drawers from the cabinets that lined the walls.

This office was the nerve center of that organization. Once it was smashed, the Silencer would be crippled, discredited. Covertly, Wentworth looked around the place for a means of escape. There was no door in the enclosure in which he and the other applicants sat; no way out except that by which he had come or by the doors at the farther end of the main office—which would mean running the gauntlet of all those desks.

One by one, he studied the clerks, while an idea began to take shape in his mind. There, at one side of the big room, was a man who seemed to be a supervisor to whom the others brought their finished work. He was about Wentworth's size, and his face would be easily duplicated—

At that moment, he got up from his chair and walked across the office to a lavatory—and Wentworth went into action.

Shuffling through the gate in the wooden railing, he went up to one of the desks and asked directions to the washroom. The hard-eyed clerk grunted, and nodded over his shoulder. Blinky squinted for a moment and then slouched over to the door. But the moment he stepped inside, and closed it after him, all his sluggishness disappeared.

With a panther-like leap, he was across the little room, and his fist lashed out to the jaw of the man he had watched. Stunned by that blow, the fellow reeled back against a wash basin—and Wentworth followed through with a punishing blow to the body and a perfectly timed uppercut.

Catching the sagging body before it slumped to the floor, he dragged the unconscious man into one of the toilet booths and went to work without losing a second. Swiftly he stripped off the fellow's suit, his shirt and tie, and donned them in place of his own shabby outfit. Out of the lining of Blinky McQuade's coat came a compact make-up kit, a steel mirror that he propped up against the limp body... and in a few minutes Wentworth's skillful fingers had transformed his features into a perfect counterpart of those of his victim.

CONFIDENTLY, HE strode back into the office and sat down at the supervisor's desk, to take a freshly arrived stack of cards from one of the clerks. Each of those cards, he saw at a glance, was indexed with the name of a man or a woman. Each was dated, and bore a transcript of a telephone conversation. On another part of the desk lay a pile of cards, clipped together in little packets—a sheaf of telephone conversations in each, attached to a master card containing the personal history and financial standing of the telephoner.

The names on those cards read like the pages of the *Social Register,* Wentworth noted as he riffled through them—names of many of the wealthiest and most prominent people in the city. And the conversations tabulated beneath them were damning—a word-for-word record of indiscreet admissions that never should have been voiced....

Steadily, those cards flowed up to his desk, a torrent of telephone messages, telegrams that had been decoded—thousands of cards on which the day's conversation of the whole city seemed to be recorded. Name after name startled him—and then he picked up a clipped-together packet that fairly burned his fingers.

The name on the top of that was Nita van Sloan!

There, in full detail, was her personal history. With it was a record of nearly a dozen telephone conversations with Harold Trumbull, a married man and the head of one of the largest brokerage concerns in the city—amazing, damning telephone conversations that exposed her mercilessly to blackmail!

Wentworth's eyes narrowed, and his jaws tightened. All too clearly he understood the meaning of that record. Nita was on the trail of the Silencer. Deliberately, she had laid herself open to his telephone snoopers, offering herself as bait.

Wentworth watched his opportunity, and slipped them into his coat pocket the moment he was unobserved, and then went to work on another stack. Different cards, these—like the one on which Blinky McQuade's name had been recorded when he was interviewed. There were more than thirty of them, cards bearing the names of a collection of the city's worst thugs and killers—and among them was one for Owen Gleason.

Beneath the rubber band, which held them together, was a slip of paper bearing the date of the following day and a cabalistic notation, *12—53—7*. Wentworth stared at the numbers and tried to penetrate their significance, but they meant nothing to him, Twelve—fifty-three—seven. Again and again, he repeated them, juggled them—until suddenly a warning sixth sense put him on his guard!

He was being watched. He could fairly feel suspicious eyes probing him. One of the clerks from a near-by desk was coming toward him, bringing what looked like another manager. The fellow was pointing at Wentworth's coat pocket—and Wentworth realized that he must have been observed secreting those cards with Nita's telephone conversations....

THE TWO were almost up to his desk now, others turning around to stare curiously. The manager's eyes were cold and hard. His right hand was reaching up toward his vest—when suddenly he staggered back as a shower of index cards caught him full in the face, momentarily blinding him. The instant those cards left his hand, Wentworth sprang from the desk in a flying leap that sent him crashing into the terrified clerk and bowled the fellow out of the way.

Twin automatics in his hands, Wentworth whirled on the snarling clerks. Right and left, his weapons flailed, cracking down on heads, battering into faces, spitting lead at a burly thug who shied a heavy glass inkstand at him. It took the ambition out of the others, sent them scurrying back to the protection of their desks—but guns were edging over the desk-tops as Wentworth reached the doorway.

Even as he yanked one of the doors open, the shots broke out behind him. Lead whistled past his head, and the glass panels of the door shattered into thousands of pieces. Crouched low, he hurled himself out into the hallway and paused to send a warning bullet back through the broken pane.

"Come on!" his taunting invitation jeered at them. "Who's going to be the first through this door?"

But there was another door just around the corridor, and he could not possibly defend them both at once. Swiftly, he catfooted down the hall to the elevators, punched at the button, and stood with ready guns covering his back track—to fling himself into the car the moment the door opened.

The operator's eyes goggled, and he backed away from the controls. But Wentworth's gun jabbed at his ribs. Now an alarm bell was clanging out in the corridor. Angry voices were yelling, as footsteps pounded toward the elevator bank. A red light started flashing in the car.

"We're going down—express to the ground floor!" Wentworth's prodding gun muzzle added emphasis to his command. "And if anything should happen to this car you'll never operate another."

Like a shot, they torpedoed downward, to bring up with sickening suddenness as the air bank slowed the car at street level.

"Out—you, first!" Wentworth clipped, and behind the trembling operator he stepped out into the lobby—to whip a bullet at the starter, as that worthy opened fire from behind a pillar.

A howl of pain from the operator, a yell of terror from the starter as he flung himself, head first, into the shelter of a candy and cigar booth—and then Wentworth was across the lobby, out of the building, running to a corner cigar store and a telephone.

He made it.

"Take down this address, Kirk," he snapped, the moment the commissioner's voice came over the wire, "I've located the Silencer's headquarters. In the Walden Building, on Seventh Avenue and Fortieth. The fifteenth floor—camouflaged as the Interborough Employment Agency. You can round up the whole outfit, if you get here in a hurry—"

But Kirkpatrick had not waited to hear any more. The telephone clicked and was dead, and Wentworth knew that the news was already flashing all over the city from headquarters. It seemed that he was hardly out of the booth, when he caught the wail of distant sirens, and, by the time he was back in front of the Walden Building, police cars were converging on it from every direction.

In the crowd, Wentworth spotted Captain Martin, of the local precinct, and attached himself to him. They were in the second relay that shot up to the fifteenth floor. But when they sprang out into the corridor it was filled with policemen who were milling around uncertainly, like firemen who have answered a false alarm. The broken-windowed doors of the dummy employment agency were standing open, but now the big office was dark except for a high, lamp-lighted desk at one side, where two hunch-shouldered, green-eye-shaded bookkeepers seemed to have been at work on their ledgers.

These two, and the janitor of the building, were in the center of a knot of questioning officers.

"I don't know what's going on here!" the janitor protested. "A couple minutes ago, these men call me and say there's a drunk raisin' hell in the hall. When I get here, he's gone—and the doors are all smashed. And then, all of a sudden, the place is full of cops!"

Wide-eyed, he gasped his amazement, as the elevators steadily added to the blue-uniformed horde. Wentworth edged his way past and stepped into the office. At a glance, he saw that the place had been transformed. The filing-cabinets were gone, the heaps of cards on the desks had disappeared. Even before the police combed the place, he knew that they would find nothing of any value. Everything incriminating had been cleverly disposed of, and now the establishment seemed to be just what it pretended to be—an ordinary employment agency.

CHAPTER 9
GOLDEN LOOT

KIRKPATRICK HARDLY seemed surprised. He was so accustomed to failure in his efforts to cope with this criminal scourge that the miscarriage of this latest hope was just another in a succession of disappointments. Yet, he could not conceal the discouragement that rode him, or his desperation.

"This kidnaping is becoming worse—it's the last straw, Dick," he confided ruefully. "Anyone who tries to raise a hand against the Silencer is gagged immediately—either by blackmail or by having one of his family seized and held as hostage. It's getting so bad that even the newspapers are toning down in their editorials against him for fear of his reprisals against the publishers." He shook his head.

"He has the city in the palm of his hand," Kirkpatrick cursed bitterly, "He's blackmailing the underworld, as well as the wealthy—that's the answer. Their secrets are all his, and, with the threat he holds over them, he is forcing desperate killers to obey him as meekly as if they were children. It's awe-inspiring, terrifying—the tremendous power he is building up. Nobody is safe from it; nobody is secure—"

Nobody… A chill of apprehension ran down Wentworth's back like a drop of icy water, as he thought of Nita. Nobody was safe from this criminal colossus… yet she was pitting her wits against him, trying to trap him….

As soon as he could get out of the building and to a telephone, he dialed her number. There was no response. Nor was there any word from her at Sutton Place, when he talked to Jenkyns. Did that mean that she had already contacted the Silencer— that she was being held somewhere, a helpless prisoner in his devilish hands?

Beads of perspiration came out on his forehead at that dread thought, and his firm jaws clenched until the muscles at their corners stood out, hard and solid. Systematically, he tried to locate her, telephoned every place where she might be, everyone who might have seen her. As he repeated his tireless questions, the black hulk of the coin phone seemed to mock him—to take on the evil personification of the Silencer, himself.

IT WAS almost dawn before he was ready to admit failure. Wearily, he stepped into an all-night lunch wagon and ordered a cup of coffee, while his constantly churning thoughts mulled over his problem. From the beginning, he rehashed it, recalled every little item that might afford a clue to Nita's whereabouts. The Silencer's headquarters, the stacks of cards, the rubber-banded bundle with that meaningless notation....

Twelve—fifty-three—seven... Those figures had been going through his brain all night. Try as he would, he could not break them down, or penetrate the significance that lay behind them. Twelve—fifty-three—seven....

Two young fellows at the other end of the counter were joking and laughing, chatting about ships. Sailors, Wentworth noted as he glanced up at them—and suddenly understanding began to dawn upon him. The meaning of those apparently abstract numbers was clear!

"Wonder if you fellows can tell me where I'll find Pier Fifty-three?" he interrupted, as the sailors started to leave.

"Fifty-three? Sure, buddy," one of them supplied readily. "That's the Lunard Line—foot o' West Twelfth Street. I used to be with the Dorgan Line. Docked right next door, at Fifty-two—"

That was it! The '53' was the number of a pier; the '12' the number of the street on which it was located—and the '7' must be the time at which those killers were to congregate. Seven in the morning or at night? Morning, undoubtedly—that was the time liners generally docked. Seven o'clock in the morning—and the date was tomorrow... was today, for it was after five, and the sky was already brightening from dawn-gray to blue!

Thirty of the worst killers in the city converging on Pier Fifty-three, when a liner was about to disgorge its passengers... Wentworth could not imagine what sort of deviltry called for such an army of criminals—but he resolved that he would know before the thing came off!

From the lunch wagon, he hurried across town to the pier. The Lunard docks were closed up tight. Not a sign of life about them. For nearly an hour he waited, but nobody came to Pier Fifty-three or left it. Something must be wrong. Nervously, he glanced at his watch. It was a quarter to seven. Fifteen minutes more....

Out of the corner of his eyes, he noticed a taxi stopping a little farther down the street. Four men piled out of it. Others were coming from across the street on foot, walking out to the small open docks that lay between Pier Fifty-two and the Lunard layout.

Stealthily, Wentworth followed them. At the side of one of those docks was a tugboat, smoke coming from its funnels. The newcomers were climbing aboard. Now others were arriving—and among them he spotted Owen Gleason!

That was the rendezvous—aboard that tug!

From farther down the pier, a longshoreman came slouching. Wentworth watched him, a silent prayer on his lips. The roustabout passed the tug, came on. In a moment, he would be abreast of a small freight house on his way out to the street....

Unsuspecting, he approached the building, slouched past—and an automatic barrel came down on his thick skull. Without a sound, he wilted. Wentworth's arms were around him, before he crumpled to the ground, dragging him back behind the freight house. Hastily, Wentworth stripped off the fellow's filthy dungarees and torn jersey, got out of his own clothing and into the longshoreman's costume, even down to the thick-soled,

In less than a minute, the Spider was
in virtual command of the tug.

ill-fitting shoes. With frantic speed, he worked on his face, dirtying it, coarsening it, matting his hair so that it poked out grimly from beneath the roustabout's wreck of a cap.

Stuffing a twenty-dollar bill into the fellow's clenched hand, he slouched out onto the pier and walked to the tug. Its deck was crowded with men who stood around awkwardly—killers. NOW A bell was ringing in the wheelhouse. Two of the hands were on the pier, loosening the ropes and tossing them to others on board. Wentworth took advantage of their preoccupation to slip down a short companionway into the deckhouse. Nobody was there, but toward the stern he spied a locker with the door half-open. It offered a good hideaway, and, as the tug started to pull away from the pier, he had cleared a space large enough for his body between piles of rope and supplies.

Before he dived into this hiding-place he dared a glance through the porthole. The tug was headed up-river, steering a course well away from the shore. Just in time, he dived into the locker as several of the gunmen poked their heads inquisitively down the companionway.

Wentworth caught snatches of their conversation. It had to do with a boat—a liner, he gathered. The killer who seemed to be in charge was giving last minute orders, chuckling over the surprise "them damn spigs" would get. In the cabin sounded the click of mechanism being snapped into place. Wentworth leaned forward until he could see between two large boxes. Half a dozen thugs were putting tommy-guns together, filling them with ammunition.

Now the tug began to lose headway, nosing its way toward shore.

With their machine guns couched under their arms, the killers filed up the companionway. A new stillness had settled over the boat.

Warily, Wentworth stepped out into the cabin. Through the porthole he could see the killers were lying prone on the deck, hugging the gunwales. From the shore, it must look as if the tug carried nobody beside her regular crew. That shore was now less than a hundred yards away.

The little boat was working its way toward a large covered pier at which a liner was just being docked. Several other tugboats were puffing around her, jamming her into her berth. Her whistle blew a long blast, as her stay-ropes went overside and were fastened on the pier's stanchions. Wentworth saw the gangplanks rolled into place. Then the passengers were filing down onto the pier.

The tug was warped in against the end of the pier. Over the edge dangled two ropes. These were caught by the crew, made fast. One by one, a dozen thugs slipped over the side, swung up onto the pier and disappeared in the milling crowd of passengers and their welcoming friends.

FOR FIFTEEN minutes, the pier shed was crowded. Then the last of the passengers straggled off, stevedores and the liner's crew unloading the cargo from her hold. Now that the shed was fairly empty, Wentworth noticed that there was an unusually large number of police at hand. The pier was fairly dotted with their blue uniforms.

Out of the liner's hold was coming a steady stream of heavy metal bars—gold bars, bullion! On the pier it was piled in orderly rows, crossed and crisscrossed, as the inspectors checked it—a growing mound already worth millions of dollars. As that precious pile mounted, the alert guards drew in closer to it, as if to hide it from predatory eyes, to shield it with their bodies.

Hands ready on revolver butts, their watchful eyes scanning the pier, they were ready for any trouble—except what happened. Suddenly, the whole pier rocked under the blast of a terrific explosion. Stevedores came hurtling from the gangplanks. Dazed policemen stared around the great pier shed, as if they expected to see it come crashing down on their heads. But that deafening detonation had not come from the pier. It had taken place in the hold of the liner, and now clouds of smoke were pouring out of the open cargo hatches.

The ship was on fire!

The moment the astounded crew realized what had happened, they rushed below to fight the blaze. Undecided, the guards stood beside their treasure mound, wide eyes staring at the fiery tongues leaping from the hatches, as the liner started to settle at the bow. Then hell, itself, broke loose from a dozen points on the pier!

From behind pillars and piled-up baggage, submachine guns chattered, their blazing muzzles sweeping the cleared space in front of them, mowing down the surprised guards like grain before keen-bladed scythes. Guards and police writhed all over the pier, as those death-blasting muzzles turned from the piled-up corpses around the bullion mound and hosed a withering leaden stream.

With the first rattling blast, the thugs on the tugs leaped to their feet and swarmed up onto the pier. Guns in hand, they dashed for the liner's gangplanks, callously wiping out of their path any luckless member of the crew they encountered.

Like a well oiled machine, the hideous plot worked. One moment, all was confusion; next, the raiders had everything under control. While those chattering tommy-guns on the pier swept the shed, checking all opposition, others on the ship swept the decks and hatchways, while their fellows trundled the last of the gold bars from the blazing hold. It was done.

Lining up like a bucket brigade, they passed the bullion bars from one to the other. In a steady stream, that mound on the dock melted and flowed into the tugboat at its edge!

WITH A coil of rope on his arm, a bucket in his hand, Wentworth went up the companionway and out on deck. Unmolested, he walked to the gunwale and pulled himself up on the pier, to leave his dummy burden behind as he headed for the nearest gangplank of the liner.

The alert eyes of those watchful machine-gunners were paying no attention to the river end of the pier. Their work lay in the other direction where the police were making a pathetic attempt to organize opposition. Nobody paid any attention to Wentworth, as he went up the gangplank and dived into one of the ship's salons. By now, the liner was keeled over perilously but he balanced himself against the wall as he rushed down a corridor and into the first stateroom he found.

He went to work the moment he had latched the door behind him. Make-up kit spread out before him, his flying fingers performed a miracle of facial transformation. The grimy face of the pseudo-stevedore began to disappear… become incredibly ugly. His cheeks became haggard, deeply lined, his skin sallow, unhealthy looking, teeth discolored. Evil, glittering eyes peered out from beneath bushy black eyebrows. A wig of straggly, matted hair went in place over his head, the lank ends hanging down over his forehead and around his ears.

Quickly, he stripped off the stevedore's sweater and then unfastened a flat package that had been strapped tightly around his body. Out of it came a long black cape and floppy, wide-brimmed black felt hat that drooped dismally around his face.

With a final glance into the mirror, he unlatched the door—and it was as the Spider that he stepped out into the corridor—the Spider who had his chance!

FROM THE doorway of the salon, his automatics barked twice, and the tommy-gunners, who were still stationed on the liner, staggered to their feet and toppled headlong, one over the side and the other head-first into the cargo hold his weapon had been covering.

Before the echo of those shots had died away, the Spider was scurrying back along the corridor, hurrying toward the ship's stern, which now was climbing out of the water at a crazy angle. Creeping out onto the deck, he saw that the looting was almost completed, and that the tommy-gunners on the pier were blasting vengeful lead at the salon door from which their mates had been killed. Nearly all that stack of golden bars had been transferred to the hold of the tug. It would take only a few minutes more to finish the task, for the killers to back their way to the end of the pier and follow their loot....

But suddenly a black shape appeared at the liner's rail—a twisted, gnome-like creature.

Like a great bat, that eerie creature came sailing through the air—to land with stunning force, feet first, on the crouched form of a startled tommy-gunner. Even before he scrambled to his feet, the Spider's guns were blazing, sending quick death to those other machine-gunners. Totally unprotected from this rear attack, they died over their guns or flung themselves to the floor in utter panic.

Not until his automatics were empty did he snap them back into their holsters and grab up the tommy-gun at his feet. Then he sent its blasting lead into the busily working line of thieves.

As that blazing weapon chattered its song of death, the Spider was speeding toward the end of the dock, weaving crazily from side to side, as bullets began to whistle around him. For a moment, he was silhouetted on the edge of the pier. Then he sprang to the deck of the tug, the tommy-gun clearing the way before him, as he leaped to the top of the deckhouse and swiveled the weapon from side to side.

Those startled looters fell where they stood—nearly a dozen, still clutching the bars of precious metal that had driven them mad with avarice. The survivors dashed frantically for shelter or leaped overside into the security of the river. In less than a minute, the Spider was in virtual command of the tug. But he knew that he could not hold his position there on the open roof of the deckhouse. Already, bullets were seeking him as the thugs on the pier edged up to its rim and dared momentary exposure for a quick shot.

He hosed the pier with warning lead, swept the sides of the tug with another blast to keep those in the water who had gone overboard. Then he leaped to the deck, to dash into the deckhouse companion-way with his useless weapon. It was empty, but those thugs on the pier didn't know that. Their respect for the gun would keep them off the boat until he could reload his automatics....

But that deckhouse wasn't empty!

Out of a dark corner, where he had been cringing, came leaping a terrified figure. Waving a revolver over his head and mumbling something incoherent, he charged like a madman.

Wentworth was almost carried off his feet by that frenzied rush. The weapon roared within an inch of his face—and then again as its barrel clubbed down at him wildly. Desperately, his fist lashed out at the fellow's jaw, staggered him. But that crazily waving gun was firing again, recklessly spitting lead in every direction. The man was mad with fear, gibbering with utter terror—far more a menace than if he had been sane and deliberate.

The useless tommy-gun had dropped from Wentworth's hands, the moment he stepped down the companionway. Now he managed to draw one of his automatics. Warily, he circled the panic-stricken thug. Then his arm lashed out, and the automatic barrel crashed down through an eggshell-brittle skull!

For an instant, the light from the porthole flashed on the

wild-eyed face, as the fellow crumpled and slid to the floor. Then Wentworth glimpsed the countenance of Owen Gleason! QUICKLY, WENTWORTH knelt beside the gambler, raised his head. Blood was running in a bubbling stream from the battered skull. Gleason's eyes were closed, but now opened again. Sanity flickered back into their depths.

"You haven't much time, Gleason," Wentworth urged. "Only a few minutes left to square things with the rat who had Lenore murdered."

Gleason's eyes widened, rounded, and a wistful softness came into them.

"I—I *did* love her," came from his hardly moving lips. "He double-crossed me when he did that—murdered her because she wouldn't pay blackmail. I hated his guts when I found out, but I couldn't help myself, Spider. I had to do what I was told— just like the others. If I didn't, my own number would have gone up."

"But *who* is he, Gleason?" Wentworth urged, fearful that death would still that weak voice before it could make the all-important revelation. "Who is this Silencer?"

"Keller." The name was hardly audible, and Wentworth bent low to catch the faint words that followed it. "Nobody is supposed to know... but it's being whispered around... that he's Warner Keller. I had it from somebody that knows him...."

The uproar outside drowned out the rest of it, but the words had become so indistinct that Wentworth could not understand them anyway. Gently, he lowered the gambler to the floor, and

103

knew that he was dead before his shoulders touched the planking.

The thudding of feet on the deck outside brought Wentworth up from his knees and across the little cabin to the porthole. Hastily, he jammed fresh clips into his automatics as he peered through the tiny window. Desperation was making bold those thugs on the pier, driving them down onto the tug, as the police and guards closed in on them. Next, they would be storming down the companionway, seeking a place of refuge. There was a way to stop that.

Smashing out the porthole with an automatic barrel, he sent two bullets into them. That stopped the rush. Before the harried thugs had time to choose between the two evils that confronted them, the door of the companionway opened and the Spider crouched in its frame. His automatics blasted with more telling effect than the deadliest machine guns!

Miraculously, the deck cleared, and the remaining thugs on the pier turned to throw up their hands and surrender to the police.

From the open doorway, Wentworth vaulted to the deck and leaped to the river side of the deckhouse. Crouching in its shelter, he ripped off the black hat and cape, the Spider's straggly wig, tucked them away beneath the stevedore's sweater. Quickly, he worked over his face, obliterating as thoroughly as possible the ugly features that had driven such terror into the hearts of the Silencer's routed thugs.

A swift glance at the pier, where the police were now in complete command, then he slipped over the side. He swam underwater, until the tugboat was well in his rear. Past half a dozen piers he made his way downstream and then climbed out on a dock at which a freighter was being unloaded. Staggering groggily, he lurched past the foreman. He grinned inwardly as the fellow cursed him for being a drunk and ordered him off the pier.

Once out on West Street, he hailed a taxi, pressed a sodden bill into the hand of the hesitant driver and gave the address of Blinky McQuade's tenement. There he would be able to get out of his wet garments and change into respectable clothing before he hurried to police headquarters to learn Kirkpatrick's reaction to the Silencer's first defeat.

WITH A grin of anticipation, Wentworth strode into the commissioner's office. Instead of the exuberant Kirkpatrick he expected, he found his friend wallowing in the depths of dejection.

"From the look of your face, anyone would think the Silencer had just walked off with police headquarters!" Wentworth jested. "Maybe I didn't quite understand that news broadcast I just heard."

"I know—we spiked his attempt to snatch five million dollars in gold bars that were shipped here from Barcelona," Kirkpatrick admitted with little enthusiasm. "There again… every precaution had been taken to keep that shipment secret, and yet he knew just when it would arrive. He'd have gotten away with it, too—except for the providential interference of someone who sounds to me suspiciously like the Spider."

Shrewdly, he eyed his friend, but Wentworth's face was attentive, interested—and totally unrevealing.

"Yes, we spiked that, Dick," the commissioner fairy groaned, "and, within twenty minutes of his defeat the Silencer struck back. *He kidnaped Mayor Wallace's wife!* Not only that but he sent this warning token addressed to the mayor and me."

Across his desk, he shoved a pasteboard box such as is used for medium-sized bottles of toilet water. When Wentworth lifted the cover, the severed hand of a woman confronted him! It was a slender, perfectly manicured left hand, with a diamond-studded platinum band on the ring finger!

"That's the hand of Mrs. William Thornley—identified by her husband," Kirkpatrick snarled. "She disappeared yesterday. When the mayor saw that, he almost collapsed. He gave orders that tie my hands completely—we can do nothing whatever that may imperil his wife's life. We've got to sit back and let the Silencer do as he pleases."

This outrageous threat had effectively put the police out of the fight. Now it was up to the Spider to carry on alone—even though at that very moment Nita van Sloan was probably a prisoner in the fiend's merciless hands, a hostage to be disfigured and mangled at his will....

CHAPTER 10
SILENCER'S END?

NITA VAN SLOAN'S cheeks were crimson as she whispered, "Good-by, my darling," into the telephone and lowered the instrument to its cradle. Never in her life had she held such conversations with a man, but Harold Trumbull was playing his part beautifully, his every word seemingly an insinuation forcing her into arranging an illicit rendezvous....

Somewhere along that wire, she was convinced, listening ears were eavesdropping on every word, jotting them down to relay them to the Silencer. Sooner or later, he must snatch at that bait. She was sure she would hear his voice on the wire.

On the second day, the summons came. She realized it the moment she lifted the receiver to her ear and heard the unctuous yet steel-hard voice.

"Miss van Sloan, I find that you have been very indiscreet," it said. "There is a certain Mr. Trumbull involved—a married man with a devoted wife and family. Mistakes of that sort are expensive, Miss van Sloan—if one wants to keep the world from knowing of them. In this case, your folly will cost you twenty-five thousand dollars. Either that, or I shall feel compelled to get in touch with Mrs. Trumbull and acquaint her with the situation. I feel certain, too, that Mr. Trumbull's business associates will be interested—especially as a good deal of unpleasant newspaper publicity is likely to result. And you, I am sure, will appreciate what effect the revelation of your amour will have upon Mr. Richard Wentworth."

"Oh, no—no! You can't do that!" Nita gasped. "That would ruin him—ruin us all! You *can't* do a thing like that! I'd—I'd *kill* myself, if anything like that happened!"

"You should have thought of that sooner," the voice spoke dryly. "Death is a way out—but death, Miss van Sloan, is terribly final. It is easier to pay. Twenty-five thousand dollars is my price."

"I'll pay—I'll do anything if only you'll guarantee me your silence," Nita's words were low, barely more than a hoarse whisper, as if she feared that the very walls around her might be eavesdropping on her dread secret. "Just tell me what to do."

In detail, he told her how the money was to be prepared, how delivered. She took down his instructions with eager, trembling fingers.

This was the very information she wanted—that which the entire police department had been striving so unsuccessfully to obtain! With it, she would be able to bait the Silencer into the trap that would start him on his way to the electric chair! But, to accomplish it, she would need Commissioner Kirkpatrick's cooperation....

Quickly, she slipped into street clothes and went out. She hailed a taxicab that had just delivered a passenger farther down the block.

Steadily, the cab worked its way downtown... and then something seemed to be wrong. Puzzled, she leaned toward the window. The driver was heading too far east. She knocked on the window. She tried to open it, when he did not hear her. It would not budge.

"Center Street!" she called, as she rapped again. "You're taking me out of the way!"

The driver did not turn. Straight ahead, he stared, impervious to her shouting and rapping as if deaf. He bore east, straight for the crowded slums. Impatiently, Nita yanked the door.

The door would not open. The air in the cab—heavy, thick—was making her drowsy. She had to pant for breath. Invisible fingers seemed closing around her throat, choking. Her senses began to swim dizzily.

The cab was running along a squalid street, peopled with impossible-looking wrecks of humanity. Vaguely, the noises of traffic became a dull roaring in her ears. Then she knew that the cab had stopped, that she was being lifted out. She was carried down steps into the darkness....

Gradually, her senses began to return. Long breaths of fresh air gulped into her aching lungs—stale, damp air. She was being carried across a cellar into a dank, dimly lighted cavern peopled with moaning captives!

Before she had a chance to make out their faces, she was dropped unceremoniously to the floor, and a heavy metal door clanged shut behind her... to leave the prison cavern in pitch darkness!

"**THAT LETS** you out, Kirk." Richard Wentworth shoved the Silencer's grisly warning back across the commissioner's desk. "Your hands are tied. The wily devil has scored again—at the very minute you could have closed in on him and nabbed him."

Bleak-eyed, Kirkpatrick listened to Wentworth's account of his visit to Steckel's home in Adalia and the finding of the inventor's body in the deserted tenement house.

"More than that," Wentworth concluded, "I had a talk with Owen Gleason. His testimony bears out the Steckel evidence. It all points, irrefutably to Warner Keller—and Keller has disappeared. I couldn't locate him all day yesterday, and I tried again this morning. Nothing stirring—he's gone into hiding."

"Officially, I can't do a thing, Dick." Kirkpatrick squirmed in his chair. "I've given the mayor my word that the department will keep hands off the Silencer. But, as a private citizen, I'm in this thing with you to the finish! I've promised to lay off the Silencer—but not off Warner Keller!"

As he spoke, he reached for his phone and summoned four of the most reliable men on his personal staff.

"Warner Keller, general manager of the telephone company, has dropped out of sight," he told them when they were gathered in his office. "We believe he is hiding out somewhere in town, and want to know where. Send out a call for him—no general alarm. I don't want him to know that we're looking for him, and I don't want anyone else to know it, either.

"If Keller is in the city, those fellows will find him," he assured Wentworth, after they had left. "I'll call you, as soon as there is anything to report."

That call came sooner than Wentworth expected. He had hardly reached Sutton Place, when his telephone rang.

"Success," Kirkpatrick's voice spoke cautiously over the wire he feared was tapped. "Come down, and we'll go visiting."

NITA VAN SLOAN

The visit, Wentworth discovered, was to be paid to the Rose of Picardy, a night club, where, Kirkpatrick's men had reported Keller maintained an unofficial headquarters. An unpretentious establishment which affected a French atmosphere, the place had no police record and was perfectly law abiding, so far as Kirkpatrick's information revealed.

"But Keller is in there now, and we're going to have a talk with him," he concluded, as he reached for his hat.

No matter how fine a reputation the Rose of Picardy enjoyed, it regarded with disfavor callers who arrived at noon. At first, there was no response when Wentworth and Kirkpatrick rang the bell and hammered on the door. Then a burly clean-up man opened it, cautiously.

"Place closed," he grumbled. "No serve lunch."

Abruptly, he started to close the door, but Wentworth had thrust his foot through the opening. The moment the fellow saw that, his face twisted into a snarl and his big brogan stamped down, viciously. But a hard-knuckled fist lashed out and clipped him on the jaw—just as Kirkpatrick hurled himself against the door, and sent it wide open.

"Down, Dick!" Kirkpatrick shouted the warning.

Wentworth flattened himself almost as quickly as his unconscious opponent—just in time to miss the bullets that lanced at him from two doorways.

Kirkpatrick was tight against a wall, returning the fire from one of those guns, and then Wentworth's automatics were in his hands, filling the hall with their thunder. Lead slapped into the wall just over his head, thudded into the unconscious body that partly sheltered him. Then he was on his feet, leaping across the ornate lobby in pursuit of one of the killers who had fled.

Halfway across the main dining-room, Wentworth brought him down, leaped over his body and raced to the rear of the room, where a door had just slammed shut. Twice, Wentworth hurled himself against the stout panels, but they would not yield.

Then Kirkpatrick was at his side, smashing at the door with a heavy chair.

"Blast out the lock!" Wentworth clipped, and his automatic hammered away at the surface just beneath the doorknob.

Kirkpatrick's gun joined in the bombardment, and, in less time than a minute, the wood was chewed into splintered pulp. Shoulder-first, Wentworth launched himself against the door once more—and, beneath his impact, the heavy latch on the other side tore out of the weakened wood. With a rending snap, the door flung open, as Wentworth hurtled into a pitch-black room.

Flame lanced out at him, the instant he was silhouetted against the light of the dining-room. Lead ripped at the shoulder of his coat—and only his half-tumble prevented it from finding his heart. Crouched low behind an overturned easy chair, that must have been barricaded against the door, he held his fire.

To move or dare a shot, meant death from that ready gun muzzle. Nothing to do but wait, and hope that the fellow's nerve would crack....

But before that could happen Kirkpatrick took a hand in the deadly game. From out in the dining-room, his gun blasted shots through the doorway, thudding into the rear wall of the room... but drew no answering fire from the wary gunman. Half a dozen times, lead streaked through the darkness. Then, suddenly, a flaming ball of paper whisked around the doorway and landed in the middle of a flat-topped desk.

With a scream of rage, a diabolical face reared behind that

desk, plunged forward as a hand batted the illuminating ball to the floor—and in that split-second Wentworth fired twice.

THE MOMENT the wounded man sprawled headlong on the desk, Wentworth was up from the floor, snapping the electric light switch and springing to his side. Keller was fatally wounded, and knew it. Fear of death flared in his eyes, and his hands clutched at Wentworth's arm.

Kirkpatrick stood by and glared down at him, contemptuously.

"Too bad you're such an infernally good shot, Dick," he spat. "Because of that, Mr. Silencer will cheat the chair—and I've never known a murdering crook who better deserved to burn."

Keller quailed under that bitter denunciation. "I've been the goat in this," he whined. "Those murders and wholesale robberies—they were none of my doing. I may be a thief… if taking money away from those who can afford to lose it is thievery. But I'm not a cold-blooded murderer—"

"You *are* the Silencer?" Wentworth cut in, as he tried to stop the blood pouring from Keller's wounds.

"Yes—I am the Silencer!" A surge of boastful pride seemed to give the dying man fresh strength. "It was my brain who created him. My plan built up the fortune that I took away from fools who don't know how to hang onto their money. Poor fools who rush to the bank in panic the moment they are threatened with having their rotten lives exposed! But that's all I did, Wentworth—I swear it. The rest of these horrible crimes are the work of criminals who are using me as a cloak to hide under. Everything that is done now—every murder and hold-up—everything is blamed on the Silencer...."

His eyes half-closed, and his throat constricted as if the clasp of death were already upon it. Anxiously, Wentworth propped him upright and struggled to keep the breath of life in him—for just a few seconds more.

"Where is Nita van Sloan?" he spoke into Keller's ear. "Where is Nita van Sloan? What have you done with her, Keller?"

Gradually, the import of that repeated question seemed to reach the failing brain. Keller's eyes opened, and the gathering mist momentarily cleared from them.

"Nita van Sloan?" he repeated slowly. "I don't know. I haven't seen her—didn't even know that she was being blackmailed. Somebody else... must be... working on her."

A spasm shot through his tortured body, and he doubled up. "You poor damn fools!" he managed to gasp; and the death rattle that choked off his words was a half-chuckle, a mocking gloat that matched the sneer which contorted his stiffening lips.

Slowly, Wentworth lowered the corpse to the floor, and then turned thoughtful, questioning eyes to Kirkpatrick. What had Keller meant by that dying gasp? Had he really been the Silencer—or was that confession all pretense to cover someone else and give him the dying satisfaction of tricking the men who had caused his death?

"A rat to the end!" Kirkpatrick read that question in his eyes and answered it. "Couldn't even go to hell with the truth on his lips. He was the Silencer, all right. With his dying breath, he tried to trick us—but this time he is silenced for good."

Perhaps—but Wentworth wasn't quite satisfied. Those first statements of Keller's, when his initial panic still gripped him, had had the ring of truth. Perhaps, this was the end of the Silencer. Fervently, he hoped so. But an insistent voice in his brain—one of those sixth sense hunches which had so often guided the course of his life—whispered that the end was not yet. And, almost as soon as he walked out of the Rose of Picardy, he knew that he was right.

AT THE corner newsstand, he picked up an early afternoon paper and skimmed through it, while Kirkpatrick hailed a taxi. Then he spotted an item that riveted his attention. The story was from Adalia, Missouri, and headlined—

INVENTOR'S FAMILY FOUND
MURDERED IN FARMHOUSE

Her suspicions aroused by three strangers living in the home of Herman Steckel, a farmhouse on the edge of this village, Freda Ruppel, a niece of the inventor, went to the police this morning. According to her story, she had come to pay a visit to the Steckel family and was amazed to find the house inhabited by strangers—an elderly woman who posed as Mrs. Steckel, and a younger man and woman who pretended to be her son and daughter.

Escaping from them with some difficulty, Miss Ruppel told her suspicions to the police and later returned to the house with Chief Clyde Bradshaw and three of the local constables, only to find it locked up and deserted. On her insistence, entry was forced and the house searched. Seemingly, the Steckel family had packed up and left precipitately. Nothing about the place appeared suspicious until the investigators reached the cellar, where they uncovered three bodies buried under the dirt floor. The bodies proved to be those of the real Mrs. Steckel and her son and daughter. They had been dead, the coroner judged, for at least forty-eight hours.

Herman Steckel, it is believed, left for New York....

Dead for at least forty-eight hours—that meant that they had been murdered, Wentworth realized, immediately after he had started to Missouri by plane! Therefore, the three who had been so helpful to him, when he arrived there, had actually been impostors, murderers, deliberately planted there to direct his suspicions against Warner Keller!

Once more, he recoiled from the ruthless barbarity of this murdering monster who called himself the Silencer. Clearly now, he saw through the diabolical scheme. He realized how Herman Steckel and his whole family had been slaughtered, how Warner Keller had been betrayed and sent to his death— just so that the Silencer might go on unhindered until he had entrenched himself so firmly that he could laugh derisively at any attempt to cope with him!

CHAPTER 11
THE DEVIL'S EARPHONES

WARNER KELLER was dead, but the Silencer still lived. Wentworth gloomily admitted that this was about all that he had learned.

117

Patiently, Wentworth combed the day's long list of crimes, arrests, accidents, as they came in at headquarters, scanning each entry for a trace of the Silencer's manipulation. At last, he was rewarded. It was the report of an accident that caught his attention—two telephone-repair men who had been injured and removed to a hospital.

Half an hour later, a taxicab had delivered him at the uptown station house and he was talking with the desk sergeant.

"A case of too much hooch, I guess," the desk man grinned. "Funny, though, those telephone trouble-shooters are a pretty sober bunch—don't have much trouble with them. These two, it seems like, went over there to Lexington Avenue and Seventieth Street to locate a break in the cables. They got the manhole open, but, instead of going down and attending to their business, they started to hit the bottle. Several witnesses saw them whooping and staggering around the street. Then a car came sailing around the corner hell-bent, so's not to miss the light, and plowed right into them. Nearly finished them."

"Have you held that driver?" Wentworth wanted to know. "Made any investigation of him?"

"No—the dirty louse!" the sergeant cursed. "One of these hit-and-run rats. Never even stopped to see whether they were alive or dead."

There was nothing particularly significant about that—the sort of accident that might happen any day of the week. But Wentworth decided to investigate. On Third Avenue, he located an outfitter who supplied him with a jumper, overalls, cap and wide leather belt such as telephone linemen wear. A hardware store added a pick and powerful flashlight. With the pick over his shoulder, he walked to Lexington Avenue and located the manhole at the corner of Seventieth Street where the accident had occurred.

Jabbing the end of his pick into one of the holes, he lifted the cover and laid it to one side, bent over the opening and peered down into it. But before he could reach down and lift out the iron guard rails, to stand around it, an arm was thrown over his shoulder, and he caught a whiff of alcohol.

"Steady—steady does it!" a shaky unsteady voice cautioned, and he found himself coping with a tipsy individual who had almost tumbled into the uncovered hole.

" 'S a shame—holes like that in the street," the inebriate scolded. "Saved my life, you did—coulda busted my neck fallin' in there. Saved my life—that's what you did."

From his coat pocket, he drew a half-filled pint bottle of Scotch whisky of an excellent brand and pressed it on his savior.

"Have a drink," he urged. "Have a drink—have all you want. That's the least I c'n do f'r the man who saved my life. Needn't be afraid of it—best whisky you c'n buy," he assured earnestly when Wentworth waved the bottle away. "Have jus' a little drink, anyway."

"Sorry, my friend," Wentworth refused. "I'm not drinking today. You'd better come back here on the sidewalk, before a car hits you."

As he spoke, he took the fellow by the arm and led him to the curb, then turned to go back to the unprotected manhole. But, as he did so, he caught a flash of the inebriate's face—a face from

Wentworth's automatic barked deafeningly and sent flying

slugs of lead into the charging, green-clad monsters!

which all sign of drunkenness had disappeared. It had become hard, vicious—the ugly mask of a cold, gleaming-eyed killer! WENTWORTH WHIRLED and swung in one motion. His fist smashed into the snarling face, just as a gun roared from the killer's hip. Only the jolt of that unexpected blow spoiled what would have been a perfect shot. Wentworth, throwing himself to one side as his fist landed, almost felt the lead kiss his cheek.

The second shot echoed the first, and, as he dived to one knee behind the base of a light pole, he saw his second antagonist hunched in the doorway of a store on the opposite side of the street. That deathtrap was double-triggered, one gunman backing up the other so that there would be no chance for a slip-up— no chance for anyone to get down into that manhole....

Cold fury gripped Wentworth. Now he knew that he was on the trail of the Silencer!

The killer across the way was firing again, and the fellow Wentworth had knocked to the sidewalk was up on his knees, swinging his gun down. Wentworth's automatic roared, and the man in the store-front stumbled out onto the sidewalk and sprawled on his face. Lead rang against the metal of the light post, as the snarling thug behind him fired at Wentworth's back. Then Wentworth's automatic was blasting sudden death for the second time in as many seconds.

There was no weapon in Wentworth's hands, when he picked himself up from the street. Like a scared rabbit, he bolted for the open manhole and flung himself into it. He hooked the heavy cover with his pick, dragged it into place above him.

That deadly exchange had taken less than half a minute, from first to last. It was too short a time for any observers to have obtained a coherent idea of what had happened; Wentworth doubted that anyone had seen him firing. To anyone watching, it must have appeared as if the telephone-repair man had been caught, an innocent victim, in the crossfire, as two gunmen shot it out on the street. The bullet-torn bodies of the two thugs should be all necessary to establish that theory....

TENSELY, WENTWORTH clung to the rungs of the metal ladder in the manhole, and listened. It was dark there, the only light drilling in through the air holes in the cover.

Suddenly, he tensed!

His sharp ears had picked up a different sound that sounded like a distant splash.

Stealthily, he descended the ladder, until his feet touched water, then came to rest on something solid. He dared a flash of his light, found himself standing on the floor of the tunnel through which the telephone cables were laid. At the manhole, there was a sort of station, with room for men to stand upright and work. Beyond this spot, the tunnel was little more than three feet square, barely large enough for a man to crawl through in going from station to station. The bottom was flooded with dank-smelling, slimy-looking water.

Uptown or downtown? Gingerly, he lowered himself to his hands and knees, staring into the blackness. Once more, he caught that faint splashing sound, coming from the downtown tunnel!

His fingers closed around the flashlight at his belt, but he did not dare use it. With infinite caution, Wentworth began to make slow progress down that cramped tunnel—foot by foot, through blackness that was impenetrable, chill water that set his teeth to chattering. It was hard work.

His numbed hand slipped on a patch of slime, and he almost fell headlong! The tunnel echoed with the splash! The splashing ahead of him was also unmistakable, and so near now that he seemed to be almost on top of it!

Straightening up as best he could under that low roof, Wentworth grabbed his flashlight and his other hand held to the comforting butt of an automatic. His finger tensed on the trigger. Then he stared in amazement at a weird-looking creature not more than twenty feet away from him!

It was a creature covered from head to foot by a suit of some slimy-green, rubbery sort of material. The head was enveloped in a hood, with tubes running from the ears to a machine now clamped over the heavily insulated telephone cable. Like a creature from another world, that weird apparition crouched there in the tunnel, blinking into the beam of the flashlight. Only the eyes, peering out of wide, round goggles in the hood, revealed it to be a man—and the hand that streaked for the heavy revolver holstered at his side.

Grimly, Wentworth pressed the trigger. Three times the narrow tunnel reverberated with thundering explosions, and the leaden slugs buried themselves in that outlandish-looking costume. When Wentworth shoved the automatic back into its holster, the man in that freakish outfit lay sprawled in the water.

Curiously, Wentworth bent over him and examined his

covering. The hood, he discovered, could be detached from the rest of the costume. When he removed it, he recognized the swarthy face beneath it as one he had often seen in the Bit House—a killer.

THE MACHINE, to which the tubes were attached, was much like an old-time phonograph. A box-like arrangement about two feet long and one foot square, it clamped tightly around the telephone cable and was held in place with straps. The top, under a transparent cover, consisted of an intricate system of wheels that operated a revolving cylinder to one end of which an apparatus, something like a reproducer, was attached. At the other end of the box was a dial similar to that of a radio.

Here was a find!

Wentworth slipped the hood over his head and tinkered with the dial. For a few moments, he could hear nothing—and then a woman's voice was speaking, talking to another woman whose daughter was ill. His fingers turned the dial a bit farther—and an angry man's voice was complaining because some delivery was two days late.

One after the other, he listened in briefly on a dozen telephone conversations, and still there were more whenever he moved that dial the slightest bit farther. By some incredible feat of engineering, Herman Steckel had perfected a machine so sensitive that it could tune in on any of the two hundred or more wires in that cable without even breaking the insulation and attracting the attention of the central office.

Wentworth took off the hood, bent closer to examine the intricate mechanism more closely... then quickly snapped off his light. The vault-like stillness of the tunnel had been broken. A variety of noises were echoing through it—noises that seemed to come from behind him. Dimly, he heard the wail of police sirens, the sound of far-away voices up on the street.

But, muffled as they were; those voices were too plain. *The manhole cover had been removed!* A moment later, he was sure of it. Men were coming down into the tunnel after him!

"The dirty wire-tapper!" a fragmentary shout drifted down to him, and its import chilled his blood far more than the penetrating cold of the water in which he crouched.

Wire-tapping had become a deadly charge in the city during the past few days—as terrible as kidnaping or degeneracy. The terrified public, cowering in fear of the Silencer and his listening legions, were all too ready to pounce on anyone caught seemingly engaged in that crime.

Wentworth did not dare back up to that manhole and make an appearance with the captured wire-tapping machine. He knew the psychology of mobs all too well. They would give him no chance to explain but pounce on him like wolves the moment he was dragged up out of the manhole.

There was nothing for him to do but go ahead. Strapping the machine around him, so that it hung suspended under his chest, he crawled over the body of the dead listener and once more started through the stygian blackness. Block after block, he seemed to crawl.

He tensed, motionless, straining his ears to hear. Nothing but utter stillness. It *must* have been his imagination. To be certain, he switched on his light—and there in the distance stood another of those curiously garbed listeners, and another! They were coming down through the next manhole to cut him off!

WENTWORTH'S AUTOMATIC banged, sent two bullets at those green-clad bodies—and the thugs scampered back out of range in the shelter of the manhole station. They would not dare face that gun or come into the tunnel after him. Yet they had him trapped, securely bottled up between their station and the police at the other end.

"You must be lonesome all by yourself down there," one of them yelled. "We're gonna send you some company. Ever get friendly with water moccasins? Here comes a whole family!"

One of the deadly snakes writhed full in the flashlight's beam, its ugly, splotched body, suspended at the end of the tunnel by a cord. Then the cord was cut, and the wriggling killer plopped down into the water. After it came another, another—until half a dozen had splashed into the tunnel. Wentworth knew that they were already coming toward him, attracted by the light!

Desperately, he backed down the tunnel. At first, only one thought obsessed him—to keep away from those poisonous fangs. Then he took hold of himself, mastered the instinctive panic the scaly menace had inspired.

The body of the dead listener! Frantically, he scurried backward until at last his foot contacted the corpse. He climbed over it, shoving it in front of him, bending the legs back at the knees and stretching it across the floor of the tunnel to block the way as effectively as possible. There was no current in that stagnant water, and he prayed that the moccasins would not leap over his human bulwark but sink their venomous fangs into the dead flesh.

Slowly, cautiously, he pushed the body along in front of him, fearful every moment that a blunt, arrow-shaped head would come lancing at him over the top. If he could manage to work the cadaver up to the manhole, where those murderous thugs waited to hear his death screams, he might be able to use it as a shield. If he could shoot his way out of the trap in which they had penned him….

But before he reached the distant manhole, the beam of his light revealed a slight indentation in one side of the tunnel, a square sort of door which he had passed in the darkness on his previous trip. At first, when he pressed against it, nothing happened. Then, when he hunched his shoulder and put his full weight behind it, the concrete slab yielded, pushed inward until he could crawl through the opening—to find himself on the floor of a cellar. Evidently he had stumbled upon one of the ways by which the listeners entered the tunnel.

Closing the entrance after him, he flashed his light around the littered cellar until he located a stairway. The door at its top opened, when he tried the knob, onto the rear of a lower hall-way. Dripping wet and begrimed from wallowing in the filthy water of the tunnel, the wire-tapping machine unstrapped and tucked beneath his arm, he went to the street door and glanced cautiously up and down the avenue.

A block away, the street was crowded with excited people—a mob held back on the sidewalk by a cordon of police. Another knot of officers and detectives was gathered around the opened manhole through which he had gone underground. Instead of going down into the cable tunnel, they seemed to be passing long hoses into the manhole.

Curious to know what they were doing, Wentworth hailed a taxi and ordered the driver to go ahead slowly. As he passed the open manhole, he saw that the hoses came from tanks that were attached to a pumping-machine—tanks of gas intended to drive him up from his supposed underground sanctuary.

A red light halted the cab and he crowded as close to the side window as he dared.

"You're sure he's down there, are you?" a skeptical police official was demanding of somebody. "A fine bunch of chumps we'll be, if we find you've been having a pipe-dream. All right, come on!"

The voice that answered amazed Wentworth.

"No fear of that, captain," it said confidently. "I saw him go down. He's rigged out like a telephone-repair man, but that's only a fake so that he could get down there to the cable."

And as the taxi started again, Wentworth stared back incredulously at the speaker—young Phil York, Mabel Rice's fiancé!

CHAPTER 12
CITY OF THE DEAF

O NCE WELL past that crowd, Wentworth changed the taxi's course and headed for police headquarters. On the way downtown, he turned on the radio and tried to pick up a news broadcast. When he tuned in the municipal station, he found what he wanted—and far more.

"Mayor Wallace has issued a general alarm for the arrest of Richard Wentworth, whom the police have identified as the wire-tapper who was seen entering a telephone manhole at Lexington Avenue and Seventieth Street a short while ago," a special bulletin was being announced. "This man, who is a crack shot, is wanted for the murder of two men who were guarding the manhole where two of the company's repair men were mysteriously injured earlier in the day. When last seen, he was disguised as a repair man. All members of the police force are warned to be on the lookout for him and to arrest him on sight."

Wentworth switched off the radio and sat back in the seat, tight-lipped, hard-eyed. Easily enough, he could understand what had happened. Frantic with worry over his kidnaped wife, Mayor Wallace had been stampeded into issuing that order—had gone right over the head of his police commissioner in his unreasoning anxiety.

Somebody had revealed Wentworth's identity to the police, deliberately made him a fugitive—and that somebody undoubtedly was Phil York. Phil York… Wentworth remembered how he had discovered the clerk running away from the house in which Giles Norton lay murdered; how he had found York trailing and spying on him in Holian Alley… He remembered, too, that it was Mabel Rice who had sent him to the deserted tenement where he had found the body of Herman Steckel….

Was it possible that these two were members of the Silencer's organization, that they had been following his orders in everything that they did?

There was only one safe place left for Richard Wentworth—the miniature fortress he had constructed in the rear of Sutton Place. His people must be warned of the danger so that they would be prepared for a surprise attack.

Stopping the cab at a corner drugstore, he stepped into the telephone booth. Instead of Jenkyns, the voice of Ram Singh answered his call. Wentworth grinned with satisfaction. Quickly, in Punjabi, he outlined the situation and told the Sikh what to do—gave him swift orders until the line suddenly went dead. It had undoubtedly been cut, but the disconcerted wire-tapper had not thought and acted quickly enough.

Wentworth's grin widened, as he pictured the fellow's confusion when that unintelligible jargon came to his ears.

By now the cab was within a few blocks of its new destination, and Wentworth watched alertly from the window as it swung from a side street into Sutton Place. The street was quiet, almost somnolent in the deepening dusk. But just as the taxi came to a stop in front of the apartment house, Wentworth's sharp eyes caught a movement in the shadows across the way. A shifting shadow was edging toward him from another direction—another, still another.

"Flat on your belly on the floor!" he warned the startled driver, as he opened the door—and then slammed it shut again, immediately.

Like metal drawn to a magnet, bullets thudded into that taxicab, a deadly hail that seemed to beat upon it from every direction. Half a dozen thugs were rushing in, converging upon its lone defender—but before they reached it, half of them went down. Death struck at them not only from the cab window but from both sides of the apartment-house doorway. Instead of facing a single gun, it seemed that a dozen were trained on them.

In mid-stride, the survivors halted and tried to retreat. One started back—only to spin around dizzily and fall on his face. Another dropped his weapon and howled with agony, as he clutched his arm and dived back the way he had come. Thirty seconds after that intended surprise attack had begun, it was all over, and the only unscathed killer was diving thankfully around the corner he had thought he never would reach.

"Good work!" Wentworth complimented, as Ram Singh sprang to open the taxi door and Jackson, his chauffeur, anxiously inquired whether he was all right.

"Pick up this contraption—" he indicated the wire-tapping machine—"and lug it inside, while I settle the damage with this driver. Quick, too—here come more of our friends!"

AROUND THE corner swept a large sedan, its windows open. Before the sub-machine gun, that poked from it, began to chatter, Wentworth was through the front door and racing across the lobby with Ram Singh and Jackson. Once they were behind the metal-sheathed door of the rear apartment they were secure against any attack, and could take their time about going through the bedroom closet and along the subterranean passage to the stronghold in the rear.

Clearly, the Silencer had now marked him for death, leaving no loophole for his victim to escape. Already, he must have heard of his men's failure; and, already, Wentworth knew, others must be coming to take their places. With the unlimited number of criminals at his command, the new lord of the underworld would be able to throw a cordon of killers all around the block to spike any attempt to get away....

Experimentally, Wentworth picked up the telephone. As he expected, the line was dead.

Thoughtfully, he turned away from the useless instrument and considered his plight. Cut off, by an army of thugs, from any possibility of leaving the block, he was being isolated here, his very attempt to communicate with the outside world frustrated.

But there was another means of communication the cunning devil had overlooked—the radio. Wentworth maintained an amateur station sufficiently powerful to reach any part of the country.

He went to it and turned on the receiving set, then nodded with satisfaction. It was operating, bringing in the usual chatter of the enthusiastic amateurs.

And then Wentworth heard it—a voice that came in boomingly. It was talking to him!

"Wentworth... Wentworth... calling Richard Wentworth," it followed up his regular call letters.

"This is the Silencer, Wentworth," the speaker identified himself. "You have been so tremendously interested in my affairs that I felt I could not keep you in the dark about my plans. You have tried to use your telephone, haven't you? So have thousands of other people on Manhattan Island, and they have been no more successful than you. For once, this bedlam of a city is

133

completely silenced. Not a telephone is operating—and not one will be back in service for at least twenty-four hours.

"Before then, I will have had plenty of time to complete the—let us say 'financial readjustment' you thought you could interrupt. In the morning, every bank in this city will be looted! Every police car will be decoyed out of the way by faked orders and then put out of commission! The moment it opens, the Stock Exchange will be thrown into a panic—a panic that will spread from New York and become nation-wide! It will make the Silencer the supreme dictator of the country, with all-hearing ears in every town and city!"

WENTWORTH WAS stunned by the magnitude of that mad program—an outrageous program that might not be so mad with the devilish cunning and the smooth-working efficiency of the Silencer's ruthless organization behind it.

"No; I am not such a fool as you think, my dear Wentworth," the jeering voice cut in on that reassuring picture. "I am not speaking out of turn—for you are the only one who is listening to me. The moment I established contact with you, I gave the word—and the city's electric power followed its telephone service!

"You have a power plant of your own—that is why your receiver is still operating. But you will be perfectly silenced. You are not going to do any more talking—not even to the charming would-be detective I have here with me—"

Wentworth could feel the perspiration oozing out on the back of his hands, the hair at the nape of his neck stiffening, as his brain leaped to the meaning of those taunting words. And then he heard the sound he dreaded most... Nita's voice raised in a scream of pain!

"Oh, Dick!" she shouted frantically. "I know where—"

But whatever she had tried to tell him was drowned out by the mocking laugh.

It brought an icy feeling around Wentworth's heart, and made him feel as if all life had died in him.

CHAPTER 13
THE SPIDER'S STING

WHITE-FACED, RICHARD Wentworth turned away from the useless panel board and looked into the shocked eyes of the three faithful friends who had listened to every word. Jackson, Ram Singh, Jenkyns—each would have given his life for Nita van Sloan without a second thought. But now they were as helpless as the man they served. Free to walk around there in the house, but to do nothing else. To pace from window to window, all four yet were of no more use to Nita than if they had been bound and gagged.

Restlessly, he strode to a wide window and stared out over the East River. The hope that was half-formed in his brain withered and died. No chance to slip out by means of the speedy motor cruiser he kept anchored beneath one of the piers on which part of the building rested.

Beaten, discouraged, he turned to where his servants stood regarding him with sympathetic, understanding eyes... and in that desperate moment inspiration flashed in his tortured brain! A wild scheme, perhaps, but it would work—*it had to work!*

Quickly, his nimble thoughts wove the plan together, perfected it. In a few moments, it was complete. He outlined it to Jackson and Ram Singh, carefully instructing them in the parts they must play. Then they went to work....

TEN MINUTES later, Wentworth's big Daimler limousine rolled out of its private garage and down the drive to the high wall which enclosed the grounds. Ram Singh, dark-faced and expressionless, sat at the wheel, and beside him the face of Richard Wentworth, tense and tight-lipped, peered out alertly into the night. Down the street, the limousine sped—but before the Sikh could turn the wheel, to swing out into Sutton Place, a car swept up on each side of them to block the way. Pocketed securely between the converging machines, Ram Singh could only jam on the brakes as a dozen thugs closed in on them and rained bullets against the Daimler's armor-plated sides and bullet-proof windows. The car halted.

A dozen snarling-faced thugs—and in the open windows of the pocketing cars the muzzles of tommy-guns appeared! The moment those deadly typewriters began to chatter, the Daimler surrendered. Holding their empty hands above their heads, the occupants submitted silently, as the thugs swarmed around the car and relieved them of their weapons.

"Smart feller," the burly, broken-nosed thug, who seemed to be the leader, grinned as he shoved his way into the front seat and ordered four of his men to get into the rear. "I heard you was plenty tough, Wentworth—but I guess you got sense enough to know when you're licked. Okay there, Gungha Dhin," he nodded to Ram Singh. "Get goin'. We're headin' downtown. Never mind where—you'll find out plenty soon. Just head south—and be careful you don't happen to make a foolish mistake when we're passin' a cop." The automatic, resting in his lap, tilted significantly.

Ram Singh glared with smoldering eyes that were like coals of fire in his dark face, but without a word he did as he was told. Straight down Second Avenue he drove until they reached East Seventeenth Street and were passing beside Stuyvesant Square Park.

"That'll do, Gungha," the leader grunted, as his automatic came up in readiness. "We're changin' drivers here."

At his signal, men got out and bunched around the driver's door. Two of them seized Ram Singh and dragged him into the rear compartment, where they bound his arms to his sides with a trunk strap.

"You next, Wentworth," the leader grinned—and the muzzle of his automatic jabbed out to prod into the ribs of the man beside him. It was done quickly.

With the two captives helpless on the back seat, and one of the thugs at the wheel, the Daimler resumed its course downtown. Finally, it came to a stop in an odorous, thickly congested East Side street where the building line was a scarce ten feet from the curb. One of the thugs got out and lifted a pair of rusty iron cellar doors—and, when an elevated train rattled past on the corner, the two bound figures were bundled out of the car and dragged to the yawning black hole of the stairway. On the brink, they made a last desperate attempt to break loose—but their captors lifted them bodily and dived into the dark pit with them.

For a moment, after they disappeared, that little sector of the dimly lit street was quiet. Stragglers, slouching past, glanced curiously at the expensive limousine. But they could not see that the back of the rear seat, of the apparently empty car, was pushing forward ever so slightly. Cautiously, it inched outward and raised up until a pair of keen eyes were at the window level, glancing quickly up and down the street.

Then the rear cushion was flung high—and out from behind it scrambled a misshapen, spider-like, black-garbed figure that leaped across the sidewalk in a bound and dived down into the cellar!

WITH THREATENING guns jabbing into their ribs, and strong hands fastened in their collars, the two prisoners were hustled across a foul-smelling cellar toward a dim light that blinked at its farther end. Through a creaking door, they descended into another basement room that stank even worse than the one they had left—and then down into a sub-cellar, another.

It was a veritable catacombs of lantern-lit corridors and caverns, burrowed into the earth by hands long dead. Almost, it was as if they had left the modern world behind them at the street level; as if they were going back into the Age of Darkness, medieval cells and dungeons....

And the dismal sub-cellar, which finally seemed to be their journey's end, might well have been a part of the grimmest Inquisition!

Lashed to the dank pillars were nearly a dozen women, clothing half-ripped from their bodies, faces dirty, tear-stained, eyes half-mad pools of suffering.

On the grimy floor at their feet lay the twisted body of a well-dressed, gray-haired man, the lower half of his face a raw horror where the burning hand of the Silencer had eaten deep into his flesh.

Held powerless in the grip of two husky thugs, while a dozen others looked on eagerly, young Phil York stared up defiantly into the slit eyes of a black-hooded devil who stood with folded arms in front of him. Like a medieval torturer, his hands thrust into the capacious sleeves of his black robe, that shrouded fiend mouthed obscene threats. A slim, red-headed figure tore madly at the ropes cutting into her flesh, as she fought to free herself from one of those arched pillars.

"Please—oh, please!" Mabel Rice pleaded. "Don't do that to him! I'll do anything you want, if only you won't hurt him! He won't disobey again—I swear he won't! I'll stay here! You can do anything you want to me, if he does—"

Hopelessly, her voice faltered and trailed off into a choking sob, as if she realized all too well the futility of her pleas.

Nita van Sloan, her shoulders lashed securely to a pillar across the cellar from the half-hysterical girl, turned compassionate eyes on her—eyes that suddenly widened unbelievingly, and then were flooded with quick concern and terror of their own!

"Dick!" she gasped as she saw the two new arrivals being thrust through the doorway. "Oh, Dick! Can't you save—"

And then it was as if an unseen hand clapped down over

her lips and bottled up the words in her throat. Only her eyes stared at the face of Richard Wentworth, and spoke their own message. That interruption gave Phil York a momentary respite. The masked torturer turned from him to look at the new arrivals, and a derisive chuckle came from beneath the somber hood.

"So it is Wentworth!" his mocking voice boomed. "Just in time, my dear Wentworth! You have been very curious about that trademark of mine; now you are just in time to see how we apply it—before your own experience. Bring them over here where they can see," he ordered the thugs who held them. "Mr. Wentworth is very much interested, and I don't want him to miss any of this."

Then he turned back to Phil York and once more strode up to the helpless lad.

"You are a squealer, York!" came savagely from the masked lips. "You tried to double-cross me. You thought you could disobey my orders and run to Wentworth with your blabbing tongue—but you failed. You were caught, because I didn't trust you and was having you watched. You tried to talk, and for that the Silencer has only one reward—the same dose we mete out to all informers."

"You rotten murderer!" York suddenly flared, as his eyes blazed with a martyr's defiance. "I know how you're going to torture me. I only regret that I didn't go straight to Wentworth in the first place. The only reason I obeyed you at all was because I knew that Mabel was helpless in the hands of your dirty killers. I'm sorry, darling," he turned to the sobbing girl. "I thought I could save you, but I failed."

Out from the sleeve of the black robe came the Silencer's right hand—a hand that was encased in a thick, tough glove that made it look monstrous. With deliberate, tantalizing slowness, he stooped and thrust it into a bowl of acid that stood on the floor. He raised it, soaked and dripping—and reached clutching fingers for York's face!

Mabel Rice shrieked wildly and tore at the ropes until streams of blood ran down her arms and soaked her clothing. Phil York's face became deathly white; his jaws clenched... and at that moment, a gun barked deafeningly. The Silencer's hand was slapped back as if unseen fingers gripped it—unseen fingers that stabbed through the heavy glove and brought his blood spurting out to mingle with the acid!

With a grating, nerve-jarring cackle, a black-caped, black-hatted figure hurtled out of the shadows from behind one of the pillars, twin automatics in his hands blazing a thundering death chant. For a moment, the awe-inspiring apparition held them all spellbound. In that moment, one of the thugs, who gripped Ram Singh's arms, crumpled to the floor. The other screamed horribly, as the Sikh's suddenly liberated hand swept up and then down again with a long knife that imbedded itself in the fellow's throat.

One moment of paralyzing terror—and then the thugs broke in wild panic as someone yelled, "The Spider!"

The two, who were holding the man they thought was Richard Wentworth, had gone for their guns. Before they could fire, Ram Singh was upon them. Like flickering lightning, his bloodied blade darted at them, and their screams rang out above the Spider's guns.

As swiftly as it carved its way through human flesh, Ram Singh's keen blade sliced through the straps that bound the pseudo Wentworth—and Jackson grinned his thanks as he stooped to snatch up an automatic that one of the dead thugs had dropped!

THE ROAR of guns in that low-vaulted cavern was deafening, ear-splitting; the howls of stricken and dying men made it a bedlam. Death filled the air, seemingly lashing out from every corner. In the midst of that ghastly inferno, Wentworth's glittering eyes flashed anxiously to the pillar where Nita stood.

At any moment, one of those wild bullets might thud into her soft flesh. More than anything, he wanted to spring over there in front of her, to shield her with his own body—but that might only draw fire in her direction and bring death.

But already Ram Singh and Jackson seemed to have read the mind of their chief. Sweeping the thugs out of their way, they sped to her side. While Jackson turned the cleverly counterfeited face of Richard Wentworth toward the flying bullets, Ram Singh's long knife sawed its way through the ropes that held her.

The Silencer saw half a dozen of his slinking thugs trying to escape from that death cavern, had watched them get as far as the doorway—then die there. Always, the Spider's deadly guns cut them down before they could cover the last few feet to freedom. But now the Spider had his hands full while his two allies were engaged at Nita's pillar—and that was the moment the Silencer took to make his gamble.

Swooping down to the floor, he grabbed up the bowl of acid, drew it back to dash it into the Spider's ugly face—and suddenly the container burst into pieces, its vitriolic contents drenching him!

Like fire, that powerful corrosive ate through his garments into his flesh. Frenziedly, he tried to get out of the soaked robe. He tore it from his body, the hood from over his head—to reveal the red-thatched skull and terror-contorted face of John Hobey, manager of the Redemption Mission!

Not until he had rid himself of that acid-saturated robe did Hobey realize that he stood there unmasked—the identity of the Silencer no longer a secret. The Spider knew! The Spider stood there leering at him horribly, regarding him with a malevolent expression that was part contempt and part something that drove John Hobey into a berserk rage.

Like a madman, Hobey flung himself at his enemy, reaching for his eyes with that acid-soaked glove. Like a frenzied beast, he clutched at the Spider's throat, snarling and spitting in his half-mad convulsions.

But the Spider was ready for him....

John Hobey's unmasking had given him no surprise. The moment he had climbed out of the back of the Daimler and seen that it parked just off the Bowery, the answers, which had been eluding him so long, came within grasp. He had remembered how his visit to that mission on the Bowery had brought Sam Latshaw to Holian Alley, although the mission manager had claimed that he knew nothing of the killer's whereabouts. At the same moment, something else that had been plaguing him, gnawing at his mind unceasingly, had suddenly become as clear as day. That faint but unmistakable something he had noticed in the florid reformer's carriage and mannerisms—something he had seen before, in someone else....

Calmly, the Spider met Hobey's wild rush. Deliberately, he swung at the fellow's head with a gun. The Silencer dodged out of its arc, just in time—managed to sink sharp teeth into the Spider's wrist, until the automatic fell from his fingers.

With a snort of triumph, the arch-murderer reached out with that gloved hand—only to have his arm seized in a grip that closed around it like a vise. Back, back, relentlessly that terrible glove was forced back and up—until it was right in front of his own face!

With a howl of panicky terror, he tried to back away, tried to break loose and run—but the Spider pressed after him mercilessly. Together, they tumbled to the floor, but it was the Spider who landed on top. And that acid-laden glove-hand was still imprisoned, still moving slowly but surely toward the face of its wearer.

IN THAT moment, the Silencer's last vestige of control snapped. Wild screams pealed from his throat, and he threshed and fought like a creature possessed... until that searing glove closed over his mouth. It took all of the Spider's strength to hold it there, all of his weight to keep the writhing madman down... then suddenly the threshing limbs convulsed, went limp.

When that diabolical glove fell away from his face, the Silencer was silenced for good. The entire lower half of his face had been eaten away—and now the Spider was doing things to the rest of it! He was rubbing it until the florid coloring disappeared, tearing off the bushy eyebrows and head of red hair—to reveal the semi-bald cranium, the pallid and characterless face of Vincent Crosby, Warner Keller's secretary!

"There is your real Silencer!" the Spider croaked. Suddenly, his hand reached down and pressed something that gleamed against the middle of the dead man's forehead—something that left imprinted on the white skin the crimson replica of the repulsive creature that all the underworld knew and respected.

It was the mark of the Spider, a promise instead of a threat—grim warning of the inescapable reckoning that awaited all criminals!

For a moment, the glittering eyes peered out from beneath the floppy brim of the black hat—peered significantly at Nita van Sloan, who had fainted, and then at the man who seemed to be Richard Wentworth. Jackson's head nodded ever so slightly, and his arm slipped around Nita's waist—as the Spider scurried across that cavern of death and through the narrow doorway, into the darkness that must always be his element!

POPULAR HERO PULPS AVAILABLE NOW:

THE SPIDER
- ❑ #1: The Spider Strikes — $13.95
- ❑ #2: The Wheel of Death — $13.95
- ❑ #3: Wings of the Black Death — $13.95
- ❑ #4: City of Flaming Shadows — $13.95
- ❑ #5: Empire of Doom! — $13.95
- ❑ #6: Citadel of Hell — $13.95
- ❑ #7: The Serpent of Destruction — $13.95
- ❑ #8: The Mad Horde — $13.95
- ❑ #9: Satan's Death Blast — $13.95
- ❑ #10: The Corpse Cargo — $13.95
- ❑ #11: Prince of the Red Looters — $13.95
- ❑ #12: Reign of the Silver Terror — $13.95
- ❑ #13: Builders of the Dark Empire — $13.95
- ❑ #14: Death's Crimson Juggernaut — $13.95
- ❑ #15: The Red Death Rain — $13.95
- ❑ #16: The City Destroyer — $13.95
- ❑ #17: The Pain Emperor — $13.95
- ❑ #18: The Flame Master — $13.95
- ❑ #19: Slaves of the Crime Master — $13.95
- ❑ #20: Reign of the Death Fiddler — $13.95
- ❑ #21: Hordes of the Red Butcher — $13.95
- ❑ #22: Dragon Lord of the Underworld — $13.95
- ❑ #23: Master of the Death-Madness — $13.95
- ❑ #24: King of the Red Killers — $13.95
- ❑ #25: Overlord of the Damned — $13.95
- ❑ #26: Death Reign of the Vampire King — $13.95
- ❑ #27: Emperor of the Yellow Death — $13.95
- ❑ #28: The Mayor of Hell — $13.95
- ❑ #29: Slaves of the Murder Syndicate — $13.95
- ❑ #30: Green Globes of Death — $13.95
- ❑ #31: The Cholera King — $13.95
- ❑ #32: Slaves of the Dragon — $13.95
- ❑ #33: Legions of Madness — $12.95
- ❑ #34: Laboratory of the Damned — $12.95
- ❑ #35: Satan's Sightless Legion — $12.95·
- ❑ #36: The Coming of the Terror — $12.95
- ❑ #37: The Devil's Death-Dwarfs — $12.95
- ❑ #38: City of Dreadful Night — $12.95
- ❑ #39: Reign of the Snake Men — $12.95
- ❑ #40: Dictator of the Damned — $12.95
- ❑ #41: The Mill-Town Massacres — $12.95
- ❑ #42: Satan's Workshop — $12.95
- ❑ #43: Scourge of the Yellow Fangs — $12.95
- ❑ #44: The Devil's Pawnbroker — $12.95
- ❑ #45: Voyage of the Coffin Ship — $12.95
- ❑ #46: The Man Who Ruled in Hell — $13.95
- ❑ #47: Slaves of the Black Monarch — $13.95
- ❑ #48: Machineguns Over the White House — $13.95
- ❑ #49: The City That Dared Not Eat — $13.95
- ❑ #50: Master of the Flaming Horde — $13.95
- ❑ *NEW*: #51: Satan's Switchboard — $13.95

THE WESTERN RAIDER
- ❑ #1: Guns of the Damned — $13.95
- ❑ #2: The Hawk Rides Back from Death — $13.95
- ❑ #3: Gun-Call for the Lost Legion — $13.95
- ❑ #4: The Law of Silver Trent — $13.95
- ❑ #5: The Gun-Prayer of Silver Trent — $13.95
- ❑ #6: Silver Trent Rides Alone — $13.95

G-8 AND HIS BATTLE ACES
- ❑ #1: The Bat Staffel — $13.95

CAPTAIN SATAN
- ❑ #1: The Mask of the Damned — $13.95
- ❑ #2: Parole for the Dead — $13.95
- ❑ #3: The Dead Man Express — $13.95
- ❑ #4: A Ghost Rides the Dawn — $13.95
- ❑ #5: The Ambassador From Hell — $13.95

DR. YEN SIN
- ❑ #1: Mystery of the Dragon's Shadow — $12.95
- ❑ #2: Mystery of the Golden Skull — $12.95
- ❑ #3: Mystery of the Singing Mummies — $12.95